THEIR HUNGER

"What did you see?" Angela asked.

Mary opened her eyes. She shook her head. "Blood."

"Blood?"

"Blood." Mary lowered her head to stare at her bandaged hand, perhaps thinking of the blood that was now on her hands. "Most of it had been wiped away, off the concrete floor. They were careful, but not careful enough. There was still blood left to see."

"There were no bodies?"

"No," Mary said.

"Torn clothes? Bloody clothes?"

"No." Mary looked up wearily. "I think our dear classmates took the clothes with them in the green garbage bags."

"I thought you were implying that the bags contained the bodies of the two couples," Angela said.

"Hardly. The bags were not that big."

"Then the bodies— What are you saying, Mary?"

Mary looked her straight in the eye. "They're monsters. What do monsters have for dinner?"

Books by Christopher Pike

BURY ME DEEP
CHAIN LETTER 2: THE ANCIENT EVIL
DIE SOFTLY
FALL INTO DARKNESS
FINAL FRIENDS #1: THE PARTY
FINAL FRIENDS #2: THE DANCE
FINAL FRIENDS #3: THE GRADUATION
GIMME A KISS
LAST ACT
MASTER OF MURDER
MONSTER
REMEMBER ME
SCAVENGER HUNT
SEE YOU LATER
SPELLBOUND
WHISPER OF DEATH
WITCH

Available from ARCHWAY Paperbacks

Christopher Pike

Monster

AN ARCHWAY PAPERBACK
Published by POCKET BOOKS
New York   London   Toronto   Sydney   Tokyo   Singapore

This book is a work of fiction. Names, characters, places, and incidents are either products of the author's imagination or are used fictitiously. Any resemblance to actual events or locales or persons, living or dead, is entirely coincidental.

AN ARCHWAY PAPERBACK *Original*

An Archway Paperback published by
POCKET BOOKS, a division of Simon & Schuster Inc.
1230 Avenue of the Americas, New York, NY 10020.

Copyright © 1992 by Christopher Pike

ISBN: 0-671-74507-7

First Archway Paperback printing November 1992

10 9 8 7 6 5 4 3 2 1

AN ARCHWAY PAPERBACK and colophon are registered trademarks of Simon & Schuster Inc.

Cover art by Brian Kotzky

Printed in the U.S.A.

IL 14+

For Angela

Monster

CHAPTER I

IT BEGAN WITH BLOOD.

It would end the same way.

Angela Warner was on the couch finishing her third beer when Mary Blanc entered Jim Kline's house carrying a loaded shotgun. The time was close to ten; Jim's party should have been good for another two hours. Angela was having a great time. The party was the first she'd been invited to since she moved to the small town of Point the previous June. It was now late September. School had started a couple of weeks earlier, and Angela saw her invitation as a sign that she had finally been accepted into the local social scene. Especially since it had been Jim Kline who had invited her. Stud football jock Jim—possibly the most handsome guy in the school. Yet Angela had not let the gesture go to her head. She knew better than anyone that Jim belonged to Mary. Beautiful, confident Mary—Angela's best friend in the whole town.

Mary. Mary. The one with the loaded shotgun.

"Hi, Mary," Angela said as her friend burst

through the front door. A nice normal hi it was. But that was only because Angela's mouth was ahead of her eyes. When she saw the shotgun, she couldn't think of anything to add to her greeting. Her eyes followed only the gun. She watched with great interest as Mary raised the weapon and pointed it at Todd Green's midsection. Angela had only met Todd that night. He was a linebacker on Point High's football team and seemed like an OK guy. Just before Mary pulled the trigger, Angela had the ridiculous thought that Mary sure knew how to liven up a party.

Mary shot Todd directly in the belly.

The blast went right through his guts and painted the wall behind him a lumpy red. Todd groaned and slumped to the floor. A stunned silence choked the crowd of about thirty. No one moved, except Mary. She pumped her shotgun and whirled in the direction of the kitchen. She didn't go far— apparently she didn't have to. Between Mary and the kitchen stood Kathy Baker, head cheerleader for Point High. Kathy was a blond piece of cream pie. All the boys loved her, and as far as Angela had been able to ascertain, Kathy loved a number of the boys. She was young and fresh and had the face of a model.

Mary pointed her shotgun at Kathy's face and pulled the trigger. The blast caught Kathy in the forehead and took off the top of her skull, plastering a good portion of her brains over the railings of the nearby staircase. Kathy—her dead body—flew

2

backward and landed with a muted thump on the carpet.

The shocked silence thickened.

Mary pumped her shotgun once more, and her eyes, like twin lasers, searched up the stairs. Angela studied with dreamlike fascination the look in Mary's eyes. She was still seated on the couch in the living room, not far from the front door and Todd's messy remains, her empty beer can still in her hands. Mary was fifteen feet away, off to her left. Yet Angela could have had Mary's head under a microscope, she could see so much detail. Mary's pupils were wide, but not crazed. They scanned the visible portion of the second floor with fixed calculation. Mary had her mouth closed; she was breathing through her nose steadily and deeply. She had just blown away two people, but she seemed to be in total control.

Mary was not yet done.

Someone stepped to the edge of the stairway railing on the second floor and peered down. It took Angela a moment to register that it was Jim Kline. Angela's eyes jumped from Jim to Mary, then back and forth once more. Jim's handsome jaw dropped a couple of inches. A hard line appeared in the center of Mary's forehead. Angela sat up straighter as Mary once more raised the shotgun to her shoulder. Everyone else at the party continued to stand and watch and do nothing. The suddenness of the attack had to be to blame. Six seconds couldn't have passed since Mary had come through the front door. Angela was barely on her feet and stepping toward Mary when Mary pulled the trigger for the third time.

"Stop!" Angela screamed.

The shot missed. Jim had leapt back just as Mary took aim. The buckshot exploded a crater in the second story ceiling. Smoky white plaster drifted through the air. Jim was now out of sight, probably running for the nearest exit. Angela doubted he was going to make it. She watched as Mary swore under her breath, pumped the shotgun again, and leapt onto the stairway, taking three stairs at a time.

I must stop her now, Angela thought.

The stairway—made up of three right-angle sets of carpeted steps—described a rough spiral as it made its way to the second floor. As Mary scampered onto the first landing Angela was able to reach through the painted white posts of the stairway to grab Mary's right leg above the ankle. Mary tripped and crashed to her knees, momentarily losing her grip on the shotgun. Angela was smart. She immediately let go of Mary, grabbed the barrel of the gun, and began to pull it through the posts. Mary could chase Jim all she wanted, Angela thought, but if she didn't have anything to kill him with, it wouldn't matter.

It was sound strategy.

Until Mary kicked Angela in the face with her right foot.

"Don't!" Mary swore at her.

"Ah," Angela moaned, losing her hold on the gun and taking a step back. She tasted blood in her mouth and the room spun in a dizzy circle. But her vision was still sharp enough to record Mary's reclaiming the gun and continuing up the stairs. Angela literally willed her dizziness to pass. She knew she didn't have time to circle the stairway and start up at the proper place. She wasn't a big or strong girl but had always been an excellent athlete. Reaching up with both hands and springing off her feet, she grabbed the posts, and in a single fluid movement yanked herself up and over the railing. Mary was already off the stairs and running down the upstairs hallway that led to the bedrooms. She was definitely after Jim. She had pushed between a couple of petrified girls without saying so much as boo to them. Angela couldn't see Jim but assumed he had barricaded himself in one of the rooms.

"Somebody stop her!" Angela cried. The paralysis caused by the gruesome deaths had finally begun to lift. Statues were melting. A couple guys from the living room headed for the stairs to help her. The majority were running out the front and back doors, though. People were making noises—mainly gulping crying sounds. The two girls in the upstairs hallway were still in the silent whimpering stage. They weren't going to do anything to attract Mary's attention, and the guys coming up the stairs weren't going to get to Mary before she got off another shot, Angela saw.

I *have to stop her,* Angela thought again, going after her.

Mary was at the closed door at the end of the hallway, trying the handle. It was locked. She didn't waste time pounding on the door or asking Jim to open it for her. She retreated a couple of steps, pointed the barrel at the doorknob, and blew it away. The act took a couple of seconds, however, and she was just kicking the door open when Angela crashed into her from behind.

"Leave me!" Mary yelled at her as they toppled onto the floor of the master bedroom. Angela felt as if she had hold of a wild animal. They were both approximately the same size, but Mary tossed her off easily. Angela rolled on the carpet and struck her head on the bottom of the open door. Again stars swam in her vision. She caught a glimpse of Jim at the window and then one of Mary climbing to her feet and pumping the shotgun once more. Angela had to turn away momentarily to get her arms under herself so she could get up. During that moment an explosion of shattering glass from another shot rent the air.

This can't be happening!

Angela hadn't been standing so close to Mary on the previous shots. But now Mary was only four feet away, and the noise from the gun was deafening. Angela's hands flew to her ears. It was too late to block out the blast; perhaps she was trying to block out the madness.

Mary hastened to the ruined window and torn curtains and stared out into the night. Disgust crossed her features, and Angela realized that the window had shattered because Jim had dived through it—not because of Mary's shot. Mary raised her gun to her shoulder, started to pump the gun, then must have thought better of it. Jim had to be out of range. Mary whirled and stomped toward the bedroom door. Angela grabbed at her as she passed, but Mary raised the stock of the shotgun, and Angela let go, cowering beneath the anticipated blow. She slipped back down onto the floor. Yet Mary didn't hit her. She just ran out the door to take off after Jim—her boyfriend.

"God," Angela whispered. She didn't know how long she sat there on the floor. It might have been a few seconds or a few minutes later that the two guys from downstairs entered the room and helped her to her feet. They were both the color of chalk and like Angela were trembling. "Did they stop her?" Angela croaked.

The bigger guy shook his head. Angela had been introduced to him earlier, but the excitement of the evening had somehow caused her to forget his name. "She got away," he said.

"Did Jim?" she asked.

The guy shook his head. "I don't know. They both ran into the field, in the direction of the lake." The guy tilted his head to the side. A siren was approaching in the distance. "Sounds like the police," he said.

Angela took a breath and hurried downstairs. Todd and Kathy lay where they had fallen. Angela tried not to look but did anyway. Kathy's head was a lopsided red ball. The shot that had caught Todd had cut him almost in half. The blood of the victims had combined into an expanding river—it was everywhere. Angela's shoes were soaked in it.

She ran out of the house and onto the front yard. The bulk of the party was now standing in the driveway or on the lawn. Guys were throwing up and girls were passing out. Wails tore the air. Two cop cars, their flashing red lights spinning, came to a halt at the end of the driveway. Four cops jumped out. The kids who were still coherent pointed in the direction of the field.

"They went that way!" they cried.

The officers didn't know what they were talking about. Angela had yet to catch her breath, but she ran to the nearest cop. He was Asian—in plainclothes. Although he was short and lightly built, it was clear at a glance that he was in charge. He steadied her by the shoulders as she started to collapse in his arms.

"What happened?" he demanded.

"She shot two kids," Angela moaned.

"Where?"

She gestured weakly. "In the house."

"Who shot them?" the man asked.

"My friend. Mary."

"What is she armed with?"

"A shotgun."

"She's not inside now?"

"No," Angela said.

The man glanced in the direction of the field, which led to the woods that surrounded most of Point Lake. Angela knew the area well; she lived on the opposite side of the lake with her grandfather. If Jim could reach the trees before Mary cut him down, he'd have a chance. The man gestured one of the uniformed officers into the house. He listened for a moment to the babble surrounding him and seemed to understand the general situation. Several kids were describing Mary.

"Who's she chasing?" the man asked Angela.

"Jim. Her boyfriend."

"Why?"

"I don't know why. To kill him. She's already taken two shots at him."

"Is he wounded?"

"I don't know."

"How many shots did Mary fire altogether?"

Angela had to think. "Five."

"She'll have to reload," the man muttered. He motioned the other two officers to his side. "Do you know why she killed the other two?"

"No," Angela said. "She just burst into the party and started shooting."

"Do you live around here?"

"Yes."

"In your opinion, which direction will the boy run?"

Angela didn't hesitate. "Toward the south end of the lake. The trees are thickest there."

"Does Mary know that?"

"I'm sure she does."

"Can we take our cars across this field?" he asked, pointing.

"No. Right away you'd run into a couple of wooden fences."

The man nodded to his partners. They drew their guns. "Then we'll go on foot," he said. "When we get to the trees, we'll spread out, circle around." He turned away. "We'll get her."

Angela grabbed his arm. "What are you going to do?"

The man spoke firmly. "We're going to stop her."

"You can't kill her!"

"We'll try our best to have her surrender peacefully."

"But she won't surrender. Something's happened to her. She doesn't know what she's doing."

The man gently undid her grip. "She's killed two already. She's trying to kill a third. We must stop her—whatever it takes."

Angela wouldn't give up. "Then take me with you. She's my friend. She'll listen to me."

The man and his partners were anxious to get going. "Did she listen to you inside the house? No, she didn't. You can't come. I'm responsible for your safety." He turned away. "Stay here. Keep the rest of your friends together. We'll be back."

"But—" Angela began.

"Stay!" the man called back. He and his partners were already running into the field. There was no moon. It was not long before they disappeared in the dark. She'd just met the guy, but she knew he was competent. Then she remembered the resolve in Mary's eyes. The cops would probably have to kill her.

"No," Angela said to herself. "No."

Something wasn't right, besides the obvious. Mary was not crazy. Angela had only known her three months, but they'd spent a lot of time together in that period. Why, Angela had stayed at her house several times, and they'd talked late into the night. Mary was a strong girl; she had strong opinions. But she was intelligent—her eyes were open and she had plans for the future. She wasn't one to throw her life away on a wave of rash emotion.

Yet she had just shot two people.

Wasted them. Todd and Kathy. Those two in particular.

Now she wanted Jim.

Angela knew Mary and Jim hadn't been getting along lately, but from the bits Mary had dropped it didn't sound that serious. Angela had had no idea Mary wanted to break up with him, never mind blow his brains out.

Angela made a quick decision. A car couldn't cross the field, but she might be able to get to the wooded area where Mary had gone before the police did if she drove around the *entire* lake and came at it from the other side. She'd arrived at the party late. Her car was parked halfway down the block, and it wasn't hemmed in.

But how will you stop her? You've tried twice already. She could accidentally kill you while trying to kill Jim.

Angela decided to risk it—she couldn't let Mary die. She raced down the block to her brand-new dark green Toyota Camry, a present from her father to try to make up for all the pain he'd caused her by divorcing her mother. She hadn't seen either of her parents since the previous June.

The car started immediately, and Angela peeled rubber as she pulled off from the curb. At first she headed away from the field and Point Lake toward View Street—it was the only road that circled the lake. When she caught it a few minutes later, she upped her speed to seventy, the body of water on her right now. Point Lake was over a quarter of a mile across—almost a perfect circle of deep blue water. Even though her own grandfather's house sat on the shore of the lake, Angela had never gone swimming in it. The water remained remarkably cold even during the hot Michigan summer days.

She reached the wooded area south of the lake a few minutes later and parked near the water behind a grove of trees. Getting out of her car, Angela was struck by the fact that she might be in as much danger from the police as Mary. They both had short brown hair and were about the same height; the police could shoot her thinking she was Mary. Angela quickly pushed the thought away. The plainclothesman who had spoken to her wouldn't shoot without giving either of them a chance to surrender.

Angela strode briskly into the trees. The place was a favorite of hers. Only a short distance from her grandfather's house, she often went there to hike. In fact, she had been there only a week earlier with Mary. Mary had been unusually silent, as if she had a lot on her mind. If only Angela had probed her silence, perhaps tonight could have been avoided.

Angela had to fight down a sudden wave of nausea.

Todd's intestines slipping down the walls.

Bits of Kathy's brain smeared on the railing and floor.

It was too much.

"Mary," Angela whispered. "Why?" Then she raised her hand to her mouth and called, "Mary! Mary! It's me! It's Angela!"

Her voice faintly echoed back to her through the pine trees and out over the water. It was a warm night—the air strangely still. She moved deeper into the trees, away from the water, alternately jogging and walking. *This is crazy,* she thought. *Jim might not even have come this way. Mary might have already blown his head off.* Angela Warner could be next on the list. Yet Angela didn't really believe that. Mary wanted Jim Kline—she wanted him bad.

Jim and Todd and Kathy. What did those three have in common?

Jim and Todd were football players, Kathy a cheerleader—used to be. That wasn't much of a pattern. Angela felt sick when she thought of Todd and Kathy's parents hearing about their kids. It was ironic; Angela was originally from Chicago. One of the reasons she had decided to come live with her grandfather in Point for her final year of high school was to be in a peaceful environment. Her parents' wars as their marriage was collapsing had etched a deep disdain for strife into her heart. And now she was in this nice small town for only three months and saw two people killed right in front of her.

"Mary!" she called again.

A hand reached out from behind a tree and closed off her mouth.

Angela silently shrieked.

"Don't tell her where we are!" a voice hissed in her ear.

It was Jim. Angela relaxed as he slowly eased his hand off her face. He raised a finger to his lips. She got the picture.

"Is she near?" she whispered.

"I think so," he whispered back. He was breathing hard; she could smell the sweat pouring off him. He glanced nervously around. "Christ," he muttered.

"The police should be here in a few minutes," Angela said softly.

He nodded vigorously. "Good."

"What the hell is going on?"

"I wish I knew. Who did she get downstairs?"

"Todd and Kathy," she said.

"They're dead?"

Angela shivered. "They're real dead."

"God."

"She must have a reason for this."

Jim snorted quietly. "She's lost it. It's as simple as that."

"Did you see it coming?"

"No," he said.

Angela thought she heard something, but could

see nothing in the dark. "You know, maybe we shouldn't wait for the police. My car isn't far from here."

"Why didn't you say so? Let's get out of here."

They crept back the way she had come. She hoped she was going the right way. The woods looked much different at night. They came to a clearing she couldn't remember crossing and hesitated at the edge of it.

"Maybe we should stick to the trees," Angela said.

"Where's your car?" Jim demanded.

"I'm beginning to wonder," Angela muttered.

Dried grass cracked nearby. Angela froze. Jim turned around anxiously. Yet they could see nothing. He raised a finger to his lips again, and Angela nodded slightly. It could have been the wind.

Except the wind didn't manually pump a shotgun.

They heard the distinctive snap.

"Don't move," Mary ordered.

Angela was surprised Mary hadn't fired without announcing her presence. But when Mary did not immediately appear, Angela realized her friend had been too far away to get off a clean shot. She must have figured she wouldn't be able to creep any closer without their hearing her. Angela remembered the plainclothesman's comment about having to reload. Mary might have been down to her last shell.

Angela glanced at Jim. She kept expecting him to bolt, but understood his dilemma—he didn't know which way to run. Mary had spoken little, and the trees did funny things with sound; it was impossible to tell exactly where she was approaching from. Still, Angela thought, there was no point in waiting for Mary—she had made her intentions clear at the party. Angela realized that Jim must have simply frozen with fear.

"Go," Angela hissed at him.

"No," Mary said from behind them.

Angela turned in time to see Mary raise the shotgun to her shoulder. She was approximately thirty feet away and had a few low-hanging branches in her path to them. She took a step closer.

"Stay," Mary said.

"Wait," Angela cried, jumping in front of Jim, who was taking the short, rapid breaths of a man on the verge of collapsing. Mary took another step toward them.

"Get out of the way, Angie," Mary said, her voice cold.

"I'm not going to let you kill him!" Angela yelled. She spoke as loud as she could, hoping to alert the police to their whereabouts. Mary continued to approach.

"I have to kill him," Mary said.

"Why?" Angela pleaded.

"Because he's not human," Mary said.

"Talk sense," Angela said. "Think what you're doing."

"I know exactly what I'm doing," Mary said. She motioned her friend to move to the side with the

16

barrel of the gun. "Get out of my way, Angie. I mean it."

"No," she said.

Mary was angry. "You don't understand. I have to do this. This is your last chance. I'll kill you if I have to—to get to him."

Angela glanced over her shoulder at Jim. He wasn't holding on to her, but he was cowering behind her, using her as a human shield. She didn't blame him one bit. He had the meadow at his back, but it was too late to run now. Mary would cut him down before he got ten feet.

Angela was surprised he wasn't begging Mary for mercy.

Angela turned back to Mary and stared her straight in the eye. Mary couldn't have been more than fifteen feet away. There were no more branches between them.

"You're my friend," Angela said. "I don't believe you'd kill me."

Mary thought for a moment. It seemed she was on the verge of listening to reason. Angela even began to relax slightly, but then Mary's grip on the weapon tightened.

"I'm sorry, Angie," she said with genuine sorrow in her voice. "There are things in this world that are more important than friendship."

She's going to shoot. I'm going to die.

Angela couldn't believe it was really happening. She closed her eyes.

And said goodbye to the world Mary said she didn't understand.

But the fatal blast never came.

"Hold it!" a male voice ordered. "Don't move an inch."

Angela opened her eyes. Mary was still in the same spot, her head motionless, but her eyes were darting left and right. Angela recognized the voice as belonging to the plainclothes cop she had spoken to at Jim's house. But the woods could have been enchanted, because once more she couldn't tell which direction the voice was coming from. The man appeared to understand that and made no effort to come into view.

"Set the shotgun down on the ground," he ordered. "Slowly."

Mary continued to scan the area, not moving.

"Do it," the officer said firmly.

Mary took a deep breath. She had guts, even if she did have a screw loose. "I can't see you," she said. "I don't know if you can see me."

"I can see you very well," the officer said matter-of-factly.

Mary's head tilted slightly to the right. Angela had finally located where he must be standing—behind a clump of bushes near the edge of the meadow.

"There is a reason I must kill this guy," Mary said.

"Fine," the officer said patiently. "You can tell me about it once you've put down the shotgun."

"And if I don't?" Mary asked. She was definitely honing in on the bushes. Angela was worried she'd try to get a shot off into them. She was tempted to speak, to warn the cop, but surely he had to be aware of the danger.

"I'll shoot you in the head," the cop replied. "I'm an excellent shot and won't miss. Put the shotgun down now."

"I don't believe you," Mary said.

"I will give you five seconds," the man said calmly. "One. Two. Three. Four."

"Wait," Mary said. "I'll put it down."

"Good," he said. "No sudden movements."

Mary slowly crouched down, extending the shotgun out from her body. Angela was a mass of nerves. She just kept waiting for Mary to try to shoot the cop. But then all at once Mary let go of the shotgun, and it landed on the soft leaves.

"Now stand up," the officer said. "Put your hands on top of your head and keep them there."

Mary did as she was told.

The cop stepped into view, revolver in his right hand. He *had* been behind the bushes.

"Thank God," Jim whispered. He moved up beside Angela.

"No one move!" the cop shouted.

He was too late. Mary had dived behind a tree. Yet she hadn't gone for the shotgun. She didn't need it, because she had come to the party well equipped. Her right hand whipped behind her, and in the blink of an eye she was holding a pistol. Angela hadn't seen the second gun at the party. Mary must have had it tucked in her belt under her shirt.

The cop immediately hit the ground even though

Mary didn't turn in his direction. She wanted Jim dead—only Jim. She wanted it even though it might cost her a bullet in the brain. A spark of orange fire spit in Jim's direction. Every muscle in Angela's body spasmed as Jim cried and fell to the ground.

Then there came a second shot—a second cry. Mary's right hand whipped halfway around her body. Incredibly, the cop had shot the pistol out of Mary's hand. He had hit her in the hand, from the sound of it. Mary was in pain. And she wasn't alone. Jim was howling on the ground at Angela's feet, clutching his left leg near the knee. At least he was still alive. Out the corner of her eye Angela saw the cop climb slowly to his feet.

Mary still refused to give up. Regaining her balance, she dived for her fallen pistol. She squirmed through the leaves like a rabid animal. Her determination was almost supernatural. The cop rushed to her instead of shooting again, which no court of law would have blamed him for doing.

"I have to," Mary cried, and she found the gun in the dark. She picked it up with her right hand, which was definitely not working properly, and then transferred it into her left hand. Even though the cop was closer and an easier target, she climbed to her knees and pointed the gun at Jim.

But that was as far as she got. The officer moved like a cat. He belted Mary on the top of the head with his revolver—hard. Angela heard a cracking sound. Mary dropped her gun and stared up at the officer for a moment, puzzled. But she was probably already out because a moment later she toppled to the ground. The cop looked over at Angela and Jim.

"Are you all right?" he asked Jim.

"My leg isn't," Jim complained.

The man tucked his pistol in a holster inside his coat and knelt by Mary's side, checking her head. "You'll recover," he said—perhaps to all of them. "It's over."

Yet the words didn't ring true to Angela. Deep down, she had a feeling of dread. It seemed to speak aloud inside her mind with a cruel voice:

"My dear, it's only just begun."

CHAPTER II

ANGELA ARRIVED AT THE POLICE STATION THE NEXT DAY close to ten. Lieutenant Nguyen—the plainclothes cop who had saved her life the previous night—had called her an hour earlier and asked her to come in. The station was in the neighboring town of Balton, a city five times larger than Point and one tenth as beautiful. As Angela drove into town she noted a cluster of reporters gathered on the front steps of the station. Two teenagers butchered at a high school party—it was getting national play. Nguyen had warned her to drive around and come in the back way. He had told her that under no circumstances was she to talk to the media until she had spoken to him. That suited her fine. She had no desire to think about what had happened, never mind sell her story to *People* magazine.

A uniformed officer let her in the back door, and a minute later she was sitting in Nguyen's office. She had to wait a minute and took that time to study the pictures on his wall. It didn't take her long to realize Nguyen had been a captain in the

South Vietnamese Army. From the photos it looked as if he had been decorated a number of times. That made sense. Her contact with him had been brief, but he had struck her as brave. She was standing, studying the pictures more closely, when he came in behind her.

"My wife made me hang them up," he said.

Angela turned. Nguyen was a short, wiry man with a head of thick black hair, large, soft brown eyes, and a distinctive right list to his body. He had dashed into the field the previous night with good speed, but she could see now that his right leg had been injured at some time in the past. The leg might even have been shorter than his left. He noted her attention but didn't say anything. Angela blushed and spoke quickly.

"She must be very proud of you," she said.

"She is a proud lady," Nguyen agreed. He stepped farther into his office and offered his hand. "I'm happy that you were able to come down, Angela." They shook briefly; he had warm hands. "Please have a seat."

"I'm happy to still be alive," she remarked, settling herself in a chair at the front of his desk. He sat across from her. He appeared relaxed but very much in control. She remembered again how he had shot the pistol out of Mary's hand. He was no lightweight, this guy. She added, "I have you to thank for it."

"Why did you go after them when I told you to wait?" he asked, his question not demanding, just curious.

"Mary's my friend." She shrugged. "I didn't know what was going to happen."

"You were afraid she'd be killed?"

"Yes."

Nguyen nodded. "She almost was." He thought for a moment. "What you did was brave. How close are you two?"

"I only met her in June, when I moved here. But I've seen her several times a week since then. I'd say we're pretty close. How is she? I mean, how's her head and hand?"

"She spent the night in the hospital, but she's here now in a cell. The doctors say she has a mild concussion, and they bandaged her hand." Nguyen paused again and sighed. "But I know there's something wrong with her. Can you shed any light on why she did this?"

"No."

"Nothing?"

Angela gestured helplessly. She had a lump in her throat the size of an orange that wouldn't go away when she swallowed. She hadn't slept well the night before—actually she doubted she had slept at all. Guns and blood and guts—the memories were etched in her soul. She'd be eighty years old and still remember them.

"I don't know what to say," Angela replied. "Mary has been quiet the last few days, but she didn't confide in me that anything was wrong."

"The boy she was chasing—Jim Kline. He's her boyfriend, isn't he?"

"Yes. Have you talked to him this morning?"

"Yes." Nguyen did not elaborate. Perhaps he wanted to compare their stories—see if they matched.

"How's his leg?" she asked.

"He's up and around. He'll be all right. How were Jim and Mary getting along before last night?"

"OK, I thought. I mean, I had noticed that Mary had begun to separate herself somewhat from him. But she never came right out and said she was upset with him."

"What was her relationship to the two she killed: Kathy Baker and Todd Green?" Nguyen asked.

"As far as I know, she hardly knew either of them."

"But she went for those two. Is that correct?"

"Yes. Definitely. Then she went after Jim."

"Did you get the impression there was anybody else she was going to kill?" Nguyen asked.

"No."

"What do Jim and Kathy and Todd have in common?"

"I asked myself the same question last night," Angela said. "Jim and Todd are both on the football team. Kathy's a cheerleader. All three are popular." Angela had to catch herself. She was talking as if they were all still alive. She lowered her head and took a deep breath. Nguyen was sympathetic.

"It's not easy to see people die," he said.

She raised her eyes—they were damp. "Things like this happened to you in the war?"

He took a moment to answer. "You expect it in

war." He shrugged. "But it doesn't make it any easier." He looked out the window for a moment. They had a view of the back wall of a warehouse. "Do you want to talk to her?" he asked.

"Mary?"

"Yes."

She felt weak to her stomach. "She won't talk to you?"

"No. She says she has the right to remain silent. She won't even talk to her parents. She's clammed up."

"Will she be let out on bail?"

"I doubt it, but that's for her lawyer to arrange. I understand her family has money."

"Lots," Angela said.

Nguyen shook his head. "The families of her victims are crushed. Mary might be safer in jail than out. You might want to tell her that."

"You're saying they might come after her?"

"You never know."

"What else do you want me to talk to her about?" Angela asked.

"Why she did it. If she'd just tell us that, it would help."

Angela glanced down at her shoes. They were different from the ones she had worn to the party the night before. She had already thrown those away. She knew she couldn't wash away the bloodstains.

"Who will it help?" she asked softly.

"You never know," Nguyen said.

Nguyen led her to a small, gray boxlike room with painful fluorescent lights on the ceiling. He told her he'd get Mary and left her alone for a few minutes. Angela passed the time remembering when they had first met. Those had been happy days.

Angela had been in town a week. Or outside of town would have been more correct. Her grandfather's house, located on the far side of the lake from Point proper, had the body of water to keep the world away. Her grandfather was not reclusive, however. Although seventy-two years old, he had a flourishing social life. He loved women, and since there were few men his age who were capable of doing more than talking, the women *relished* him. He was in excellent health. Right from the start he let Angela go her own way, which suited her just fine. She had been walking alone in the woods on the south side of the lake when she stumbled across Mary.

Mary was dancing. She had on a skin-tight green leotard and tights and was playing her boom box at maximum volume. Angela stood and stared at Mary for several minutes before announcing her presence, but there was no rudeness in the delay. She was awestruck—Mary danced like a pro. But she wasn't an MTV clone. The way she moved between the trees—it was as if she were a Greek nymph descended to earth for an afternoon frolic. Mary was fully *alive* when she danced, filled with energy. Her dance was an art, and the interesting thing was that she did it to ordinary rock blasting out of the boom box.

When Angela finally did speak up, Mary stopped and stared at her. She immediately turned off the music, but she wasn't embarrassed or angry. She just said, "You're new here, aren't you? My name's Mary."

Want to be friends?

Mary hadn't said the latter, but she could have. She had taken Angela under her wing that very day. Angela had never met anyone with such incredible self-confidence—too cool to care about being cool. Besides being an incredible dancer, Mary could paint, sing, play the flute, and make—so she said—incredible love. Jim, she said, was the best.

Three months ago. The best.

And last night she had done everything in her power to kill him.

"I'll kill you if I have to—to get to him."

Suddenly Mary was at the door, being led inside by a uniformed officer. She sat down in a chair across from Angela. The chair was metal, bolted to the floor, and Mary was handcuffed to it with her good hand. She had already changed into prison clothes. The gray shirt and pants looked like unwashed pajamas—baggy and unflattering. Angela was appalled at the change in her friend's appearance.

Ordinarily Mary was a beauty. Her brown hair was cut short, as was Angela's, but it wasn't the same because Mary's had that extra gloss that

28

separated the blessed from the nonblessed. At least that was what Angela had told Mary not long after they'd met. Mary had been quick to disagree. Mary's eyes were large and liquid green, Angela's a simple blue. Mary was voluptuous—in a bathing suit she could turn heads a hundred yards away. Angela was slight and had trouble gaining weight, probably because she seldom ate much.

Eating wouldn't be a priority that day. Just looking at Mary took away her appetite. Mary had a huge bandage wrapped around her head, and the doctors had not spared her hair while treating her wound. They had lopped off a handful of it right at the top. Common treatment for a murderess, Angela supposed. Her right hand was bandaged to her wrist. Nguyen could shoot straight.

Mary stared across the table at her with blood-shot eyes.

"Well," Angela said.

"Well," Mary muttered.

"How's your head?"

"I don't know."

"Does it hurt?" Angela asked.

"I don't know."

"Did you sleep last night?"

"A little. Did you?"

"Some," Angela said.

"That's good. What are you doing here?"

"I came to see how you're doing."

"I'm all right. Anything else?"

"Yeah."

29

"What?" Mary said.

"You know what. What the hell happened?"

Mary shrugged. "You were there. You saw it all."

"That's not what I mean, and you know it. Why did you do it?"

Mary acted bored. "If I told you, you wouldn't believe me."

"Try me."

"No."

"Why not?"

"You won't believe me."

"Mary, you killed two people. You almost killed a third—Jim. How do you feel about that?"

Mary stared at the floor. "I feel nothing."

"Nothing? Not even regret? God, do you know what you've done to their families?"

Mary took a breath. "I feel bad for their families. I also feel regret."

Angela sighed. "I know you must."

"I regret that the cop stopped me before I could get Jim."

Angela was exasperated. "Why? What did Jim do to you?"

Mary raised her eyes to Angela's. "He didn't do anything to me."

Angela paused. "Did he do anything to anyone else?"

"Trust me, Angie. There's no point in talking about it."

"What did Jim do?" Angela insisted.

A bitter chuckle escaped Mary. "Boy, if you only knew."

A remark Mary had made the previous night came back to Angela right then.

"Because he's not human."

"Not human," Angela whispered.

Mary was instantly alert. "What?"

"You said last night that Jim wasn't human."

"No. I didn't."

"I heard you, Mary. I remember. Don't deny it. Why did you say that?"

Mary changed. No longer was she bored, indifferent, or defiant. She was pale, and her cheek twitched. She was *scared*. This in itself frightened Angela more than anything the previous night had. Mary turned away and pressed her hands to her face.

"Because it's true," she said.

Angela reached across the table and touched Mary's arm. "What's true? What did he do?"

Mary was having trouble breathing. "Horrible things."

"Tell me?"

Mary slowly raised her head. "You won't believe me," she said for the third time.

"Try me. Please? I'll believe you."

Mary chewed on her lower lip. She was thinking, but not normal thoughts. There was a faraway look in her eyes, and where those eyes were focused was not a happy place.

"Todd and Kathy," she said finally, "were not human beings anymore. That's why I killed them."

"You mean they did something inhuman? They hurt somebody?"

"I mean they were no longer like you and me."

Angela had no idea what she was talking about. "What were they, then?"

Mary's lower lip trembled. "Monsters."

"Mary?"

Mary smiled, a grotesque twisting of her face. "I told you."

"No. Tell me more. I don't understand."

Mary sat back in her chair and stared at Angela. "You want me to start at the beginning?"

"Yes."

"It'll be a waste of time."

"I have plenty of time to waste."

Mary closed her eyes for a moment. When she opened them and began to speak, her tone was changed. She spoke softly and simply, as if she were recounting a great tragedy.

"You know how the cheerleaders and the football players practice before school starts at the beginning of September," Mary said. "They meet and go through their routines and their plays. They do this every year. Well, this year you also know that I was seeing Jim. Sometimes I'd be bored and drive over to the school in the morning, just to watch the guys bang heads. I'd watch the girls on the squad work out, too." Mary shrugged. "That's when I began to get a clue."

"A clue to what?" Angela asked.

Mary frowned, as if remembering her confusion at the time. "I'd watch the guys, and notice how Jim and Todd stood out. I don't mean in a normal way. They've always been excellent athletes. What got me was that all of a sudden they were *too* good. Todd was a linebacker, and Jim the quarterback. Jim would hand the ball off to Todd, and no one could stop him. He wouldn't even bother dodging. He simply mowed down anyone in his path. Guys would crumble as if he were made of steel. When Jim would pass, he'd throw tight, clean spirals that could barely be seen. When one of his passes hit a receiver, the guy would double up as if he'd been shot. Those passes hurt, and I mean hurt. The coaches thought it was great, but I saw guys staggering off the field shaking their heads and clutching their stomachs, refusing to come back."

"That happens all the time in football practice," Angela said.

Mary ignored the remark. "Then there were the girls. Kathy was head cheerleader. I'd watch the squad practice, and they'd do some kind of pyramid thing, and Kathy would come from out of left field and vault onto the top of the other girls. She'd leap up ten feet easy. Right off the ground."

"That's not possible."

Mary went on. "I began to watch those three: Jim, Todd, Kathy. You might think that's weird. After all, Jim was my boyfriend. Of course I didn't need to watch him—I saw him all the time. But the truth was that I wasn't going out with him much. He didn't call me as he had, and when I was around him he was aloof. But that wasn't all there was to it. He had changed in some way that I couldn't explain. He would talk about the same things, but you know that feeling you get when someone's talking about something that they don't really believe in? Or that they have no interest in?"

"Yes."

"I felt Jim was just mouthing words because it was expected of him. He would hold me, he would kiss me—we continued to make love when my parents weren't around. But he wasn't with me. He wasn't there."

"So?" Angela said. "He was losing interest in you. I'm sorry, Mary, but it happens all the time. It doesn't mean he was a monster."

Mary showed impatience. "I tell you he was different, and I know what I'm talking about because I knew him. His mind, his heart—when I was with him they weren't there."

"Where were they?" Angela asked.

"Gone."

Angela shook her head. "I still don't know what you're talking about. If he acted so indifferent to you, why did you go to the trouble of watching his practices?"

"Good question. I think I went because I needed proof that he had changed."

"Mary."

"Let me go on. There was a time—I think it was about two weeks ago—that I went to practice for only a few minutes. I accidentally left my purse and had to go back for it. When I got there none of the guys were on the field, and all the cheerleaders appeared to have left also. I noticed that the weight room was still open and walked over to it. By then I had no hope left for Jim and me. I didn't walk into

34

the weight room, I peeped in, slyly. Yeah, I was definitely looking for something unusual. And I got it."

"What did you see?" Angela asked.

"Kathy and Todd and Jim were inside. They were alone, lifting weights. Have you ever seen a cheerleader lifting weights? I haven't, but I suppose that isn't so strange. But good old Kathy—she wasn't pumping a few extra pounds to give her arms tone. I saw her lift at least a thousand pounds straight over her head."

"That's impossible," Angela said.

"I know. But I saw her do it."

"You must have misjudged the weight on the bar."

"No. In fact, the bar she was using bent after she lifted it, she had so much weight on it. What do you think it would take to bend one of those metal bars? A strong girl, that Kathy."

"Were Jim and Todd lifting as much?"

"I couldn't tell. They were working the machines. But it seemed as if they were pushing the machines to the limit, without sweating. Here's something else: when Kathy made her dramatic lift, neither of the guys seemed to notice. The whole time I stood there watching them not a single word was said. The atmosphere was cold as a morgue."

Angela considered. "Anything else?"

"Yes." Mary leaned forward on the table. She had begun her tale with no hope of convincing Angela, but now she had warmed up. Now it was clear she wanted Angela to believe her. "After the incident in the weight room I began to spy on them. I noticed that they hung out together a lot. They'd go off alone to a corner of campus and talk. I also noticed that none of them ever smiled unless someone else was around. I stopped going out with Jim altogether, but I often drove over to his house at night and sat down the street in my car—waiting."

"For what?" Angela asked.

"For him to come out and play with his strange friends."

"You talk like they were vampires."

Mary's eyes grew dark. "They were worse than vampires. One night I was waiting outside Jim's house—it was after midnight—and he went out and drove off in his car. I followed him as he picked up Todd and Kathy. They went here, to Balton, to a bar. I assumed they'd be tossed out because they were underage, but they stayed inside until two o'clock, when the bar closed. When they came out they had two couples with them. The other four appeared to be in their early twenties. They were all laughing and carrying on. It was obvious to me the new people were drunk. I was sitting across the street in an all-night coffee shop. I couldn't hear everything they were saying, but I caught the words *party* and *orgy* and *warehouse*. Jim and Todd and Kathy were trying to convince the two couples to go with them, and they must have done a good job because the others got in their car and followed Jim as he drove away. I had to hurry to catch up with them. Jim headed to the edge of town. He parked in the deserted lot of a boarded-up warehouse. The others parked beside him. They were still laughing and talking out loud as they followed Jim and Kathy and Todd inside the warehouse."

"How did they get inside if it was boarded up?" Angela asked.

"Jim pried the boards off the door with a crowbar."

"Why didn't he pull them off with his hands if he was so strong?"

"I don't think he wanted to demonstrate his strength—yet."

"Those two couples must have been awfully stupid to go into a warehouse that was clearly deserted. Especially if they thought they were going to a party."

"I told you how drunk they were," Mary said. "And you know how sweet and innocent those three could look. They could pose for a picture on American values for a Christian TV station. Anyway, the point is they went inside. I stashed my car down the block and waited outside the warehouse behind a stack of crates for them to come out. They did, about an hour later. At least Jim and Todd and Kathy came out—not the others."

"What happened to them?" Angela asked.

Mary leaned an inch closer. "They were killed. Our innocent all-Americans murdered them."

"You saw this?"

Mary sat back and waved her white-bandaged hand in disgust. "Of course I didn't see it directly. I told you, I waited outside. But when Jim and Todd and Kathy emerged they were carrying those giant green plastic bags you put garbage in. They each had one thrown over a shoulder. They threw them in the trunk of Jim's car and drove off. It made me wonder. I walked back to my car and got a flashlight. I returned to the warehouse and crept inside. At first I didn't see anything. The place was empty, with dust everywhere. I called out, but no one answered. Then I saw this area on the floor. Here all the dust was brushed away." Mary stopped and shut her eyes. She took a deep breath, then another, but seemed not to let either go. Angela found herself leaning forward.

"What did you see?" Angela asked.

Mary opened her eyes. She shook her head. "Blood."

"Blood?"

"Blood." Mary lowered her head to stare at her bandaged hand, perhaps thinking of the blood that was now on her hands. "Most of it had been wiped away, off the concrete floor. They were careful, but not careful enough. There was still blood left to see."

"There were no bodies?"

"No," Mary said.

"Torn clothes? Bloody clothes?"

"No." Mary looked up wearily. "I think our dear classmates took the clothes with them in the green garbage bags."

"I thought you were implying that the bags contained the bodies of the two couples," Angela said.

38

"Hardly. The bags were not that big."

"Then the bodies— What are you saying, Mary?"

Mary met her eye straight. "They're monsters. What do monsters have for dinner?"

Angela was appalled. "They didn't eat them, for God's sake."

"I don't think God had anything to do with what they did to those four."

"Mary."

"Seven people went in that warehouse, Angie. Only three came out."

It was Angela's turn to close her eyes and shake her head. Shake it all out of her head, she wished. These awful images Mary so easily invoked. Super strength, strange appetites. All this from a girl who had killed two people only twelve hours ago. What was she to believe from such a person? Nothing— she could believe none of it if she wanted to be sane.

Mary's raving. She can't accept what she's done and she's invented this fantasy. There are no monsters.

Angela opened her eyes. "Why didn't you go straight to the police and tell them what you'd seen?" she asked.

"I wouldn't have been able to prove that Jim and Todd and Kathy had killed the two couples."

"But the people at the bar would have been able to confirm that they all left together. And you had the bloodstains on the warehouse floor."

"I did go back to the bar—but to the owner it

had been just another night of faceless people. He couldn't remember anybody. I also went back to the warehouse a couple of days later. The bloodstain had been washed away."

"By who?"

Mary shrugged. "Probably by them. I think they began to suspect they were being followed."

"What makes you say that?" Angela asked.

"It was just an impression. The next time I saw Jim, he looked at me funny."

"What was the name of the warehouse?"

"I don't know if it had a name."

"Do you know the address?"

"No," Mary said. "But I could show it to you."

"Could you draw me a map to it?" Angela asked.

"I don't think so."

Angela nodded. Mary was dodging every chance to have her story verified. It was all an illusion. "You should have gone to the police if you believed you saw what you did," Angela said.

Mary exploded. "And tell them what? That I saw a cute little cheerleader lift a thousand pounds over her head? That my ex-boyfriend eats people? I would have been shown the door faster than you could blink."

"Mary," Angela said patiently. "They're not going to show you the door now."

Mary quieted. "I had to do what I did. I had to stop them while there was still time."

"What do you mean?"

Mary was defensive. "Nothing."

"You've told me this much. You may as well tell me the rest."

"Why? I can see what you're thinking. Mary went berserk, and now she's concocted this crazy story to try to explain why."

"That's not true," Angela lied.

"It is true. I told you, you wouldn't believe me. Well? Do you? See?" Mary was angry at herself. "I must have been crazy to think you would."

"How come the two couples were never reported missing? That would have been big news in these parts."

Mary frowned again. "I don't know why. I suspect, though, that Jim and Todd and Kathy only picked up people who were passing through."

"You think they killed people every night?"

"I think they had strong appetites."

"Look, what do you want from me, Mary? All right, I don't believe your story. It's too ridiculous. If I was in your position and I told you the same thing, you wouldn't believe me."

"That's true."

"Then what am I supposed to do?" Angela asked.

"I don't know if anything can be done."

"Because Jim is still alive? Because he's still on the loose?"

Mary nodded gravely. "Yes. If he made a couple of partners, I don't know why he couldn't make another two. Or thousands, for that matter."

"Now the world's in danger of being taken over, is that it?"

Mary nodded again. "What I wanted to say a moment ago and didn't was that the day before the party I saw our happy threesome talking with Carol McFarland and Larry Zurer."

"Carol and Larry are monsters now?"

"Maybe."

"Why didn't you kill them as well? They were at the party."

"I wasn't sure they had changed. Strange as it may sound, Angie, I don't just go around shooting people because I feel like it."

"All right, let's pretend for a moment that everything you say is true. I don't believe it is, but let's say I do. What happened to these people that changed them?"

"I don't know," Mary said.

"But you must have an idea."

"I don't," Mary said. "But if Carol and Larry have become like the others, then it's an interesting coincidence. Carol's a cheerleader. Larry's on the football team."

"Why don't you tell Lieutenant Nguyen your story?"

"What for? *You know me,* and you don't believe me. What are the chances he will?"

"Nguyen thinks it might be a bad idea for your lawyer to try to get you out on bail. He fears Todd and Kathy's families might come after you."

Mary waved away the suggestion. "They won't do anything to me. Jim's the one who'll try to get me."

"Will you try to get out?" Angela asked.

"I don't know if I should answer that question."

"The answer is yes. But I suppose Nguyen knows that already, so I guess I don't have to worry about it."

"Personally, I think you have plenty to worry about," Mary said.

"Because the world is about to be overrun by aliens?"

"I don't know if they're alien. I don't know if they have the strength to overrun the world. But I have no doubt that they'll take over Point in the near future."

Angela glanced at her watch. "Is there anything else you want to add to your story by way of proof?"

"Two more points. You were there last night. You'll remember how Jim was on the second floor when I shot Todd and Kathy. You'll remember how he immediately realized that I'd go after him next."

"What does that prove?" Angela asked.

"Nothing in and of itself. But it's interesting that he knew he was to be next. You should see the significance. Then there was the way he dived out the bedroom window onto the roof, dropped twelve feet to the ground, and dashed into the field without breaking stride."

"I would dive out a window if someone was coming after me with a shotgun."

"But you'd bleed," Mary said. "You'd get hurt."

"You hurt Jim when you shot him in the leg. I'm sure he bled."

"I wonder how badly I hurt him."

"I'll ask him." Angela started to stand. "He's here at the station."

Mary reached over and grabbed her arm. Her eyes were wide, scared. "Stay away from him," she said, a note of pleading in her voice. "He's dangerous. Promise me you will."

"I rarely see Jim. I don't think it'll be a problem."

"But he'll know we talked. He might come after you."

Angela reached down and removed Mary's hand from her arm. "I'm capable of taking care of myself."

Mary sat back and smiled sadly. "That's what I thought, too."

Angela didn't know what to say. She told Mary she'd talk to her soon and left the room, leaving Mary chained to the chair. How sad, she thought. Mary had had so much potential. What a waste of a life. Angela hoped the court saw fit to place her in the hands of a competent psychiatrist rather than behind strong bars.

Nguyen met her in the hallway and led her back to his office. He offered her a seat, but she refused. He asked her what Mary had said.

"Nothing," Angela said.

"You were with her more than ten minutes," Nguyen said. "You must have talked about something."

"Nothing important. She won't talk about last night." Angela spread her hands. "I'm sorry."

Nguyen stared at her a moment. He had the

warmest eyes, and she felt guilty lying to him. But she saw no point in relating Mary's story. If Mary herself wanted to tell him, that was one thing. But Angela would have felt as if she were betraying her friend to talk about her friend's *monsters*.

Nguyen finally nodded. "That's fine, Angela." He led her to the door of his office. "We have your number, don't we? Let's stay in touch. If anything new happens, be sure to give me a call."

"I promise," Angela said. "Is Jim Kline here?"

"He left a few minutes ago," Nguyen said.

"How is he?"

Nguyen smiled. "You asked that when you came in."

Angela nodded. "You're right." She flashed a smile. "I just thought I'd ask again. Goodbye, lieutenant. Thanks again for saving my life."

"Thank you for coming in," Nguyen said.

After Angela Warner left, a uniformed police officer brought in a cassette tape and a tape player and placed them on Nguyen's desk. The officer left, and Nguyen rewound the tape to listen to the conversation between Angela and Mary. He had, of course, listened in while Angela and Mary had been in the room. If he felt any guilt about eavesdropping on the two girls, he was unaware of it. A horrible crime had been committed, and he was determined to get to the bottom of it. That was his responsibility. Angela was right about Lieutenant Nguyen—he was very good at his job.

What struck Nguyen as he went over the conversation again was not so much what Mary had said but the strength in her voice. She was not a flaky teenager. He remembered how she had stood up to him in the woods. She had more guts than most of his soldiers in the war.

But what about her story? It was preposterous, of course, but it disturbed Nguyen in ways he couldn't explain. Long ago he had learned to trust his intuition, even above reason. But what was he to do here? The boy Mary had tried to kill—Jim Kline—perhaps he was a murderer. Nguyen had personally interviewed Jim and had not liked him. The boy was hiding something. The way his eyes had darted to the left and right when he was being questioned had reminded Nguyen of a caged animal. He was guilty of a crime, of that Nguyen was sure. But Nguyen couldn't spare the manpower to have Jim followed, not day and night. He doubted he had the legal right to have the boy trailed anyway.

It had impressed Nguyen that Angela had not divulged Mary's story. Those two were friends; that had not changed with the events of last night. Perhaps that friendship could be exploited.

When the tape was finished Nguyen pushed the button on the intercom on his desk. He got one of his men, Officer Martin. The man had helped him capture Mary the night before.

"Any word on Mary Blanc's bail?" Nguyen asked.

"She won't get a hearing with a judge until Monday," Martin said.

"Can you postpone the hearing?"

"Blanc's lawyer will complain."

"They always do. Have the judge be ill when it comes time for the hearing. Ask him as a personal favor to me. I don't want that girl getting out. She's dangerous."

"I understand. Anything else?"

"I want a list of all the boarded-up warehouses in Balton," Nguyen said. "Can you get it for me?"

"Sure," Martin said. "What do you want it for?"

"I want to sweep a concrete floor," Nguyen said. "To see what I find."

CHAPTER III

THE FUNERALS FOR TODD GREEN AND KATHY BAKER were held the Tuesday morning after the Friday night shootout. The principal at Point High canceled classes for the day, and approximately one quarter of the student body attended. Todd and Kathy had been popular, and as the minister eulogized them, crying could be heard. But the families of the slain, bunched together in black in the front pews of the chapel, remained silent. Grief was etched on their faces along with hatred. Angela Warner sat at the back of the chapel and wondered if the families knew she was a friend of Mary's.

Angela didn't go to the grave sites after the ceremony. She'd had enough of grief; she didn't know why she'd come at all. Yet, deep inside, she did know the reason. It was guilt. She continued to feel she should have spotted Mary's disturbed state of mind before the shots had been fired. Of course, Mary had not acted disturbed, not even after she'd finished her murderous mission.

Angela hadn't talked to Mary since Saturday morning.

Now she was getting into her car after the ceremony. Jim Kline approached, and she felt no fear of him. She had run over Mary's story two or three times and had come to the same conclusion. Something deep inside Mary's mind had snapped. Case closed.

"Angie," Jim said. "Can I talk to you for a minute?"

Jim was what was known as a totally rad dude. God had designed his body and fit him snugly into it. Jim was tall, six two, and built like a hardy redwood. His hair was brown, always neat, and his face was chiseled. He had the broad shoulders and strong arms of an experienced quarterback. Yet his brown eyes were somehow clumsy or shy, as was his smile. He moved awkwardly for an athlete. He didn't look particularly intelligent, and that was OK, because if he'd had brains along with that body there would have been no resisting him.

Angela had always been attracted to Jim and was happy when he'd invited her to his party. She tried not to think about it now.

"Sure, we can talk," Angela said, standing beside her open car door. More than half the people weren't going to the grave sites. Her car was trapped in the chapel parking lot by at least three other cars. She wasn't going anywhere for a minute anyway. "How's the leg?" she asked.

"Better," Jim said, glancing down. "She just winged me." He looked up again, his eyes shifting to the chapel, then back to her. He seemed embarrassed. "I just wanted to thank you for what you did Friday night. You saved my life."

Angela chuckled softly. "Lieutenant Nguyen saved your life. He's the one you should thank."

"I wouldn't have been alive for Nguyen to do anything if you hadn't slowed Mary down at the house and in the woods," Jim said. "If there's anything I can do for you, ever, don't hesitate to ask. I mean that—seriously."

Angela blushed. "Maybe some lonely night I'll take you up on that. No, just kidding. Thanks. I mean, it's OK." Her tone became serious, and she sighed. "I just wish I'd been able to do more—that we weren't having these funerals today."

"Ain't that the truth," Jim said. Twin black hearses waited in front of the chapel. Soon the coffins would be loaded into them. Thankfully they'd remained closed during the ceremony. Word was that the mortician hadn't been able to do a thing with Kathy's head.

"How are the families?" Angela asked.

"Real bad." Jim gestured helplessly. "This is all so sudden. They want to strike back, but they can't."

"Mary will be convicted. There's no chance she'll get off."

"I suppose," Jim said miserably. He stuffed his hands in the pockets of his undersize gray suit and focused on his feet.

Angela touched his arm. She could feel him shaking beneath her fingers. "What happened?" she asked. "Do you know?"

Jim looked at her. "Didn't you talk to her on Saturday?"

"Yeah. But I couldn't get anything out of her."

"Didn't she say anything?"

"Just a bunch of gibberish."

"Like what?"

Angela shrugged. "I can't even remember most of it."

Jim shook his head. "What happened is I told her I wanted to break up with her and go out with other girls. She got real upset—actually it caught me by surprise. You know how strong Mary always is. So when she told me I couldn't leave her, that I belonged to her, I didn't know what to do. I avoided her at first, but she kept coming to our practices and wouldn't leave me alone. She called Todd and told him to tell her if I went out with any other girls. She cornered Kathy at school and told her if she so much as looked at me she'd kill her."

Angela frowned. "I can't believe Mary'd act that way."

"You can't believe it? She was my girl—I thought I knew her better than anybody."

"Why did you want to break up with her?" she asked.

Jim glanced once more at the hearses, the steps of the chapel. The front line of pallbearers had appeared. Jim was probably supposed to be with them. "This is a lousy place to be having this discussion," he said.

"We can talk about it later," she said quickly.

"Would that be all right? I'd like to talk about a

lot of things. How about Friday night, after the game?"

"Are you going to play Friday?" she asked, surprised.

"Yeah. My leg's fine, really. Would you like to get together then?"

Angela considered a moment. They were at a funeral—a double funeral, for that matter. Jim had been Mary's boyfriend, and Mary was her best friend. He was right; this wasn't the time to be discussing such matters. But Jim wasn't asking her out on a date—not really. He just wanted to talk. There could be no harm in that.

"Sure," she said. "That'd be fine."

Angela got home around eleven o'clock. Her grandfather was still asleep. He kept late hours when he was on the prowl for a new woman, which he had been for the last week. A week searching was a long time for him. Angela closed his bedroom door before sitting down at the kitchen table to read the paper. Mary's rampage was still front-page news. Angela had asked the police that her role in the events not be discussed, and so far she had avoided being turned into a hero by the media. She hadn't gone to school on Monday and didn't know how her classmates were going to treat her. She had no taste for the hero role, especially at the expense of her best friend and two dead classmates.

Angela had hardly settled herself when there came a knock at her door. It was Kevin Christopher, a guy from her class who lived up the road.

Next to Mary, he was the best friend she had in the small community of Point. Their friendship might have been even closer if he hadn't developed an immediate crush on her when they first met at the beginning of the summer. He made no secret of his devotion to her, which both flattered her and made her uneasy. Kevin was short, about five eight, with a mess of black hair and a grin that would light up at the slightest reference to his favorite subjects, which, of course, were sex and sex. Yet Angela believed Kevin had never had sex outside of the confines of his own head. Too much the altar boy, he was never crude, even when he was trying to be. He simply didn't have the experience to draw upon, she figured.

Not that she had any. In fact, they made a great pair, both virgins pretending they had been around the world on a waterbed. She cared a great deal for Kevin. He made her laugh, and she sure could have used him over the weekend. Yet she hadn't seen him since before the party, and didn't know where he had been.

"Am I late?" he asked as she opened the door.

She smiled, although it was forced. The funerals had taken more out of her than she had realized. "You are just in time. Come in, take off your clothes. Let's do it quick. My husband will be back in a few minutes."

Kevin jumped inside the door. "Where is he?"

"With your wife."

"The tramp."

"Really. How would you like it today?"

"Hard and fast," he said.

"Is there any other way?" she asked. Then she laughed as he grabbed her, and she pushed him away. She really didn't feel like clowning around. "Calm down, boy. My husband is asleep in the next room."

Pretending disappointment, he said, "Maybe next time."

"There's always time," she agreed. They carried on like this whenever they saw each other. It had become a ritual. But sometimes she worried if she hurt his feelings because she was the one who had to bring him back to earth. She wished she had romantic feelings for Kevin—they might even have had fun together. He was handsome enough, but he just didn't *do it* for her.

Not the way, say, Jim Kline did.

But we're not going to think about that. He's a monster, remember? He eats poor unsuspecting visitors.

Mary had a sick imagination. Maybe she could write horror books in prison and make a fortune.

"A and W," Kevin said, giving her a quick hug. "How are you?" He often called her—Angela Warner—A & W in honor of his favorite root beer. Before she could respond he let go of her and strode into the house to plop down on the living room couch. "It's nice to be home," he said.

Her grandfather's place was a two-story cedar frame built on an open plan, with exposed beams in the vaulted ceiling. The wood was heavily lacquered pine and polished cedar. A huge basement ran the length of the house. The living room's sliding glass windows opened out onto Point Lake, which was calm on this warm, sunny day. Kevin sat and glanced at the water, on the far side of which stood Point High, only a year old. It had been built directly on the shore; half the classrooms had a great view, which made bored minds wander. Angela went over and sat on the couch beside Kevin.

"Hey, girl," Kevin said, not meaning Angela. Plastic, her grandpa's collie, came bouncing into the room and shoved her head onto Kevin's lap. Angela loved the dog—she was beautiful—but Plastic had reservations about Angela. Perhaps she resented having another female in the house. But with Kevin, Plastic couldn't show enough affection. She hungrily rose and licked his face. Angela let it go on for a moment until Kevin began to lick her back. She motioned for Plastic to return to her favorite sunning spot, a wooden balcony that jutted out from both her grandfather's upstairs bedroom and her own, ten feet directly over the water. Plastic could lie on the balcony for hours, staring at the water. One would have thought she was a cat searching for fish. Yet the dog never dived in.

"Go, girl," Angela said. "Go see the water."

Plastic looked at her with her who-the-hell-do-you-think-you-are-giving-me-orders expression. But she turned and went up the stairs, nudged the slider open, and went out to sun herself.

"Smart dog," Kevin remarked.

"Yeah," Angela agreed. "She likes you more than me."

"Most young females in heat do."

"Where have you been?" she asked.

"I've been here and I've been there. And I've been in between." He paused. "Did you go to the funerals?"

"Yes. I just got back. How come you didn't go?"

"I wasn't invited to the party."

"Be thankful for small favors."

"How were they?" he asked.

"The funerals? Awful. I don't know why they bury people. I don't want to be buried."

"Do you want to be cremated?" Kevin asked.

"I want to be shot into space and dropped into the sun. Really, where have you been? How come you didn't call me back this weekend? I called you twice."

"Did you leave a message?" he asked.

"Two."

"Can I use the excuse that my machine wasn't working?" he asked.

"If you really need to. But I needed you this weekend."

Kevin appeared genuinely concerned. He was ordinarily protective of her. He reached over and put his hand on her knee. "I'm sorry. I went to a computer convention in Chicago. I didn't even know about the shootings until I got back late last night."

"How come you didn't tell me you were going to this convention?"

"Because I didn't get invited to the party."

"You said that already."

"Then it must be doubly true," he said.

Now she was concerned. "Did it upset you that I went to the party without asking you? You understand it wasn't my party. I couldn't invite people."

Kevin nodded. "It was Jim Kline's, I know. And he almost got killed at it. The word is that you saved his life."

"That's an exaggeration. The cops saved his life."

"I heard you took a bullet that was meant for him."

Angela laughed. "These stories. Does it look like I took a bullet meant for anybody?"

He studied her for a minute. "You look terrible, Angie," he said quietly.

Angela sniffed and lowered her eyes, playing with her fingers, an old habit of hers whenever she was upset. "Of course I look terrible, I feel terrible. Two people died, and Mary's in jail. I don't know. I almost feel like leaving Point and going back to live with one of my parents. They only fought with words—they didn't use shotguns."

Kevin moved closer. He put his arm around her, and Angela sagged into his side. "You can't leave," he told her. "I'll go on a rampage if you do. I'll sleep with every girl in school and get them all pregnant, and they'll have to close the place down just to save face. It would be a disaster for the whole state." He leaned over and kissed her cheek. "It'll happen, Angie dear, if you leave me."

She sniffed again and smiled, but her smile didn't last. For all her contact with both Mary and Kevin over the past summer, the two of them didn't really know each other. They moved in separate orbits.

"Mary's lost her mind," Angela said softly.

"I heard you talked to her at the station," Kevin said.

She sat back and wiped her face. "News sure gets around fast. Did you hear what we talked about?"

"No. Nobody has any idea why she did it. Everyone is waiting for you to tell them."

"If I tell you what she told me, can you keep it secret?"

"Absolutely," he said.

From experience she knew Kevin was one to keep his word. "Mary says she had to kill Todd and Kathy and Jim because they were monsters."

"I could have told you that," Kevin said with a straight face.

"I'm serious, Kev."

Kevin blinked. "Tell me the whole story."

She did, everything that had happened the night of the party, and then everything Mary said at the police station. Kevin listened patiently without interrupting. He had a keen mind; he was a straight-A student. As she spoke she hoped he'd be able to shed new light on what had happened. When she was done, she sat patiently and waited for him to speak.

"She certainly sounds like she's lost her mind," he said.

"That's what I think."

"But maybe it's not her fault."

"What do you mean?" Angela asked.

"I hesitate to bring this up. It probably won't help, but it's a theory I'm sure the papers will get to eventually."

"What is it?"

"It happened last year, before you arrived. Point High had just opened. Before, we used to take buses to Balton High. It was a pain in the ass—forty-five minutes each way, and Balton High was way overcrowded. Anyway, we got our own school, and everybody was happy until last fall, near the end of football season. That was when a group of students started to get headaches and stomachaches. There were about thirty of them, maybe more. A couple passed out in class, and it wasn't unusual for someone to run to the restroom suddenly to throw up. Everyone got spooked, and a huge meeting of parents and faculty and students was called. Experts were called in to study the school's water, the materials that had been used in constructing the buildings, even the grass and flowers that landscaped the campus. They didn't find a thing wrong, and then suddenly the problems began to diminish. Although they didn't go away altogether. The experts chalked it up to mass hysteria."

"What did they think brought on the hysteria?" Angela asked.

"They had a few theories. The weirdest one was that summer had gone on too long. We did have strange weather last year. It was November, and we still had some days in the mid-eighties. But like I said, the problem seemed to take care of itself. Yet the interesting thing was that only a certain segment of the students was affected. Your story made me remember that."

"The football players and the cheerleaders?" Angela asked.

"Exactly. I wasn't affected. None of my friends were. But I think all the girls on the cheerleading squad were. I know Kathy Baker was. I remember her mother wrote a nasty letter to the local paper saying how something at the school was poisoning her dear daughter."

"Was Jim Kline affected? Or Todd Green?"

"I couldn't say for sure. They might have been."

"Was Mary?" Angela asked.

"I doubt it. I think it was only those two groups." Kevin chuckled. "Maybe it was hysteria caused by stress. The football team lost all but two games last season. That's not unusual for a school that's just getting started, but I know the players didn't like the ribbings they constantly took."

"Did any of those who got sick act emotionally distraught?"

"Not that I know of," Kevin said.

"Then what does this have to do with Mary? The contamination theory—or whatever you want to call it—can't be used to explain what she did."

"You're looking at it backward," Kevin said. "The contamination theory could be used to explain what Mary says the others did."

"You honestly believe that they did those things?" Angela asked.

"No. As I said, it's just a weird theory. I think Mary blew a circuit and started shooting people.

It's happened before, you know. Maybe Jim was dumping her and she was upset."

"He told me he was dumping her," Angela said.

"You talked to him?"

"This morning, at the funerals." She didn't bring up the fact that he had sort of asked her out. Kevin would feel jealous.

"How is he?" Kevin asked.

"Fine. His leg is better."

"Already?" Kevin asked. "I heard she shot him good."

"That's just a rumor. She barely winged him." Angela stood and paced in front of the couch. "I don't want to drop this getting sick business yet. Are you sure the experts found nothing unusual?"

"That was the official announcement. They closed the school for a few days while they took samples of everything. I went up and watched them. They were thorough."

"Did any of the symptoms return later in the year? Like when track and baseball season started?"

"We didn't have a track or a baseball team last year. I'm not sure we'll have one this year. We're still getting the teams together. We only have a student body of six hundred to draw from. But to answer your question, I really don't know."

Angela stopped her pacing. "I just hate to accept the idea that Mary's gone bonkers." She frowned. "Maybe those three were affected by something and did do strange things."

"How did Jim seem when you talked to him?"

"Fine," Angela said.

"Did he look capable of eating anyone alive?"

Angela waved her hand. "Even Mary admitted that she never actually saw them hurt anybody."

"She was quick to blow them away with the little evidence that she had," Kevin said. "We could go check out that warehouse."

"We can't. She couldn't remember where it was."

"How convenient," Kevin said.

Angela nodded. "I thought the same thing. Hey, would you like to go to the library with me? I'd like to read more about the reports of the students getting sick."

Kevin stood. "Sure. As long as you promise me you won't leave the area for fear of catching an invisible disease."

Angela chuckled. "There's no danger of its being invisible with me. When I catch the least little thing, it always shows."

Angela had never been to the library in Point. In Chicago it might have been mistaken for a private bookshelf. It was dismally small. But they had come only for back issues of the local paper, *The Point Herald,* and there were plenty of copies available in the back, the librarian said. She was an old woman, perhaps a bit senile, and she must have been losing her sight. She was listening to a book on tape when they entered. As they knelt to collect the issues they wanted, they heard the Ghost of Christmas Past chewing out Scrooge for being such a cheap bastard.

It took them only a few minutes to find the right papers. As Angela read the articles, she discovered little new. About three dozen students had complained of being ill. Doctors were brought in and could find nothing wrong with them. Contractors and chemists were contacted. They, too, couldn't find anything wrong with the school. Then the students had gotten better, the experts had gone away, and everybody was as happy as could be until Mary Blanc had crashed a party with a shotgun and a serious attitude problem.

There was, however, one thing that Angela learned that she hadn't known before. It came out of an interview with the head of the contracting firm that had built the school. Angela called Kevin over and showed him the quote.

I lost money on the job. The foundation took us three times as long as we thought it would because the ground was so hard. Our engineers say the iron content of the soil was ten times what they thought it would be. We should have built a steel mill there instead of a high school. Maybe the geologists are right when they say the lake was formed by a meteor.

"Point Lake was formed by a meteor?" Angela asked.

"That's what I've heard," Kevin said. "At least the hole in the ground was. The water came later, of course."

"Where does Point High get its water?"

"From the lake. Didn't you know that?"

"No," she said.

"Angie, there's nothing wrong with the water. I drink it. You drink it. And there's nothing wrong with us. Besides, they tested the water inside out when the students started to get sick. It's perfectly OK."

"Is that where my grandfather's water comes from?" she asked.

Kevin thought a moment. "I don't think so. I think he gets it from a well high up on the hill, where my family gets theirs. Lots of people on our side of the lake get their water from there."

"Why get water from a well when the lake's sitting right here?"

"I don't know," he said. "Good question."

"You said that *some* people say the lake was formed by a meteor. Do other people disagree?"

"First off, it's not that unusual to have a lake—or any body of water, for that matter—formed by a meteor. They say Hudson Bay was created by a meteor long ago. But as far as Point Lake is concerned, there haven't been any studies done to be sure. Personally, I think a meteor must have formed it."

"Why does our young scientist believe that?" Angela asked.

"Because you can't get a proper reading on a compass in this town. The needles just spin. The iron in the ground here is magnetic, and meteors are often magnetic. But before we go too far with this, I must say again that the students' getting sick and Mary's going berserk has nothing to do with the water or the meteor. If that were the case, we'd all have been affected. In fact, thousands of people would have been affected for the past hundred years, since this town was built. Even before then— the Indians were here first. As far as I know, the water didn't bother them."

Angela shivered, although she didn't know why. Maybe it was just the thought of living beside a lake that had been carved out by something from outer space that made her feel suddenly chilly. She remembered again how cold the lake water always was—even in the summer.

"I suppose you're right," she said distractedly.

— CHAPTER IV —

FRIDAY NIGHT FOUND ANGELA AT THE FOOTBALL GAME. There had been talk all week long of canceling the game out of respect for Todd and Kathy. But it was finally decided that the contest could be dedicated to the two, rather than abandoned. It was the first game of the new school year, and it was against Balton High, played in Balton's stadium because Point High didn't yet have one of its own.

Angela had had an interesting week at school. Everywhere she went people talked in whispers at her back. She had dual claims to fame: she had helped stop Mary, and she was Mary's best friend. She supposed one was good and the other bad, but she didn't know if they canceled each other out. Actually, she talked to very few people all week. When she didn't see Jim Kline around, she assumed his leg was bothering him more than he had let on.

Yet Friday night he was starting quarterback.

Angela had gone to the game without Kevin. She felt guilty about that. When he'd asked her if she wanted to go to a movie, she had answered that she wanted to stay home. There was no chance he'd attend the game because he disliked football as much as he disliked football players.

Angela sat by herself high up in the stands after buying herself a couple of hot dogs and a large Coke. Mary was much on her mind, especially after she'd spoken to her parents briefly on Thursday—a difficult conversation. It wasn't as if Mary were recovering from an illness or anything. Hi, how's your daughter? How's her cell? Does she like her striped pajamas? I hear she's got a rapist for a cell mate. Yeah, that's tough when the warden won't even let her call collect. Angela hadn't known what to say. Apparently, though, Mary had yet to have her bail hearing with the judge. Mary's parents didn't know why it was taking so long. They sounded so sad, it broke Angela's heart.

The game started. Angela tried to push away her gloomy thoughts and enjoy it. Ordinarily she liked football. She pretty much liked all sports and had hoped to go out for volleyball or basketball. She was disappointed that no teams had been formed yet and might not be until after she graduated.

At a glance it was clear Balton High was the favorite. As both teams lined up for the kickoff Angela could see how much bigger Balton's players were. The reason was simple. Balton High had a student body five times Point's size. Five times as many kids to draw from. Angela stood and cheered as Point received the kickoff. She hoped it would be a good game. Point ran the ball back to the twenty-yard line, and the offensive unit, led by Jim Kline, came onto the field.

"Then Jim would pass. He would throw tight, clean spirals that you could hardly see. When they hit the receivers the guys would double up as if they had been shot. Those passes would hurt, and I mean hurt."

In the next six minutes, on the opening drive of the game, Angela watched Jim throw five complete passes, the final one thirty yards into the end zone for a touchdown. All of them were tight spirals, but none of his passes made his receivers double up in pain. He did appear to throw them hard, however, and accurately. His performance was amazing, to say the least. But Angela did not get the impression she was watching a superhuman play. In fact, she hardly thought about what Mary had said once she was into the game.

And a fine game it was, from Point's perspective. Balton might have been bigger, but they weren't as quick or as coordinated. Point quickly jumped to a two-touchdown lead. By the end of the first half the score was 21 to 7, and it seemed as if Point was just getting warmed up. As the players jogged to the lockers for the halftime break, Angela hurried down to the bleachers toward the fence that separated the stands from the playing field. Jim was one of the last players to leave the field. Three tiers up still, she was able to call down to him as he passed by. She hoped she wasn't drawing undue attention to the act.

"You're killing those guys," she said.

He removed his helmet and raised his head. Right then, at that moment, he didn't look anything like a clumsy jock. He looked more like a conquering gladiator. He flashed her a quick smile. "Are we still on for tonight?"

"I'm on if you're on," she said.

"I'll meet you outside the showers twenty minutes after the game."

"I'll be there." It was sounding more like a date all the time.

The second half was a repeat of the first half, except it was more devastating. Point ran off two touchdowns in a row before Balton could respond with a field goal. There was nothing supernatural at work. Balton was simply being outplayed, both offensively and defensively. They were also being outcoached. Only two players came out with injuries, both on Balton's side. Two was not a lot to lose in a football game, Angela thought. It was probably below average. The second player, though—hurt in a pileup in the last five minutes—did have to be carried off the field.

The final score was 42 to 9.

Jim had completed over three quarters of his passes.

She met him outside Balton's showers long after the twenty minutes he had promised. She didn't mind. He was quick to apologize and looked so handsome with his wet hair and equipment bag thrown nonchalantly over his shoulder that she considered herself lucky. She had to remind herself that the purpose of their date—she had begun to call it that in her mind—was to discuss a tragic matter. Jim, though, pumped by his team's victory, appeared to have thrown off the gloom of last week's incident.

"I think we scared them in the first few minutes," he said as they walked toward the parking lot. The night was warm; maybe they'd have another one of those long summers. "They just rolled over and played dead."

"It looked so easy I was afraid I'd get bored," she said.

He paused and turned to her. "I hope I didn't bore you."

She laughed quickly, embarrassed. "No, you were incredible. I don't see how you guys lost a single game last year with you at the helm."

"I improved a lot since last year. We all did." He added quietly, "I think playing this game for Todd and Kathy gave us an extra spark tonight."

She nodded. "I'm sure they appreciate it, wherever they are."

Jim raised his head to the stars. "Yeah," he muttered. Then he shook himself. "Are you hungry?"

"I just ate two hot dogs."

"But you haven't had dessert. Let's go somewhere to eat."

"OK." She gestured to the far end of the lot, where her car was parked. "I have my car. Would you like to meet somewhere?"

He grinned. "Afraid to come with me?"

She was glad it was dark and he couldn't see her blush. She poked him in the chest, feeling hard, smooth muscle. "You don't scare me, big boy."

They did end up taking separate cars back to Point. They met at a local restaurant called Cider Café. The game had been relatively early, six-thirty, and they were seated in the restaurant before ten o'clock. The place was upscale—there was nobody from school there. Angela remembered that Jim's family, like Mary's, had money. Jim ordered a New York steak, shrimp, a baked potato, salad, vegetables, and milk. He said he was always starving after a game. She asked for herb tea. The hot dogs had given her indigestion.

"Should we get the unpleasantries out of the way first?" Jim asked as they waited for their food.

"The shootings and Mary?" she asked.

"Yeah." Jim folded his powerful hands and leaned across the table. His dark eyes, in the light from the candle, were anything but cold. They were warm and most enchanting, and she had to consciously stop herself from staring too long into them. "I didn't tell you the whole story at the cemetery about Mary and me," he said.

"What did you leave out?"

"I told you that I'd said I wanted to go out with other girls? And she freaked out?"

"Yes."

Jim cleared his throat. "This is embarrassing. I realize now I shouldn't have been so tactless and told her who I wanted to date. At the time, though,

I thought it was better to tell her than to have her find out on her own."

Angela took a deep breath. "Yes?"

"I wanted to ask you out."

"Really?"

"Yes," he said.

"You told her that?"

"Yes."

"You shouldn't have told her that."

Jim sat back and sighed. "I know that now."

"God," Angela said. Then she blinked. Jim Kline wanted to leave Mary for her? Maybe there was something wrong with him. Her amazement forced the question out of her. "Why did you want to go out with me?" she asked.

He appeared to be stunned, then chuckled. "I like you."

"Why? I mean, you hardly know me."

"Haven't you ever liked someone you hardly knew?"

"Yes." A perfect example was sitting right across from her. "But Mary's so incredible." Angela shook her head. She was flattered and totally confused. "She must have been shocked."

Jim appeared to be disgusted. "Obviously."

His remark sobered her quickly. "Do you hate her?"

"No. Yes. I can't hate her, but I want to. Todd was my friend."

"How about Kathy?" She was already thinking about the competition.

72

"Kathy was a friend, too. We all used to go out together."

"Mary told me."

Jim's interest was piqued. "What did she tell you?"

Angela paused. Just being in a restaurant with Jim made her feel disloyal to Mary. There was no sense embarrassing Mary in front of Jim. "She said that you grew cold and uninterested," Angela said carefully.

Jim was impatient. "That happens when people break up. I thought she would have been mature enough to accept what was happening and get on with her life. What else did she tell you?"

"Nothing."

"Did you see her Saturday morning?" he asked.

"I told you I did. She refused to tell me why she did it. She didn't mention anything about you wanting to go out with me."

"I didn't mean to lay such a heavy rap on your shoulders."

"It's not your fault," she said quickly, her heart pounding in her chest. She didn't want to say what she did next, but she owed it to Mary. "Mary's still my friend."

Jim nodded. "I understand if you don't want to see me."

"I didn't . . ."

"Angie?"

"What?"

"What were you going to say?" he asked.

73

"I don't know."

"I guess this is all too quick for you," Jim said sympathetically.

She stared at the candle on the table, then back into Jim's eyes. They had flecks of purple around the irises; she had never noticed that before. Such unusual eyes. She imagined she could see the flame of the candle burning behind them.

He's too hot for me.

"I like you," she said softly.

Again he was interested. "What do you like about me?"

The body you're wearing under those clothes.

"Your piercing intellect and subtle wit," she said.

He smiled. "You're making fun of me."

She shrugged. "I just like you. You're cute."

He reached over and took her hands in his. "You're cute."

He could see the blood in her cheeks now. "Next to Mary I look like old wallpaper."

"Mary's in jail. Mary's going to stay in jail. Let's not talk about her anymore." He raised a finger as she started to protest. His tone had gone hard all of a sudden. "At least not tonight. All right? Let's have fun."

She lowered her head, feeling like Judas. "All right."

Jim's food came, and he ate. Boy, did he eat. She sipped her tea and restrained herself from lecturing him on the virtues of chewing. When he had cleared his plate he ordered dessert—cheesecake —and insisted she have a bite. He liked it so much he had a double helping, although she thought it dry.

But she liked watching him eat. Just watching him.

He paid for the meal with his father's credit card.

"What do you want to do now?" he asked as they stepped outside into the night air. The warmth of the day continued to linger, although it was getting close to midnight.

"Go to bed," she said.

He laughed and clapped her on the back. "You Chicago girls get right down to business, don't you?"

"I meant sleep." He had hit her a bit harder than she would have preferred. But he was so darling that it was OK.

He continued to chuckle. "I know what you meant. I didn't mean to embarrass you."

"We Chicago girls don't get embarrassed that easily."

"Wow. What's that mean?"

She giggled. "I'm not that tired. Follow me back to my house in your car. We can go for a walk."

"Along the lake?" he asked.

"Wherever you'd like, Jim."

Jim almost killed them both when he arrived at her house. He tried pulling in beside her in the driveway, but there wasn't room. He ended up banging her grandfather's propane tank with the front bumper on his four-wheel drive. He leapt out of the vehicle when he saw what he'd done.

"Did I break the seal on it?" he asked. Reaching inside his truck, he eased the vehicle back slightly.

Angela dashed over to the tank. Being from a city, she wasn't experienced with propane. She studied the tank in his headlights. He had definitely dented the metal, and it worried her. He joined her a moment later, touching the twisted white curve with his big hand.

"I think it's OK," he said.

"Are you sure? Should I wake my grandfather?"

"It's fine for now. If it was leaking, we'd know it. But it should be checked in the morning. If it needs to be repaired, I'll pay for it."

"It won't explode?" When she had originally moved into the house she had felt as if she were sleeping next to an atomic bomb.

"It'd take a full collision to get a tank like this to explode." Jim paused to study the length of the forty-foot prone cylinder. "But I'm surprised your grandfather has such a big tank. You usually find ones this size on a farm, where a huge barn has to be heated."

"My grandfather explained to me that until ten years ago there used to be five houses around here. They all used the same tank."

"What happened to them?"

"I think they burned down," Angela said. "You would have been eight then. Do you remember anything like that?"

"Vaguely."

"You have lived in Point all your life, haven't you?"

"Yeah." He nodded to the tank. "A big fire could have set this sucker off."

"What would such an explosion do?" she asked.

"If the tank had just been filled, it would blow away the house." He snapped his fingers. "Just like that."

"I think my grandfather just had it filled."

He laughed. "Then I'll try not to run into it again."

Angela had visions of huge explosions in her head. For no reason they excited her. "If it blew, would it make a crater in the ground?"

"What?"

"You know, like a small meteor had hit here?"

"I don't think it would do that. Why do you ask?"

"Just wondering," she said.

Angela ran inside to use the bathroom before they went for their walk. Jim followed her in. Plastic was asleep on the living room sofa. The dog didn't even stir. Naturally, her grandfather wasn't home. Jim made a joke about him and said he had quite a reputation around town. He almost sounded envious.

A few minutes later they were walking hand in hand along the shore of the lake. Angela didn't know who had reached for whom, but together felt right. Her guilt about Mary stayed with her, but she tucked it aside. She could worry about it later. Her fingers almost disappeared inside Jim's. They walked without saying much, and that was nice. A half moon hung low in the west, the silver rays glittering on the water, on the bare skin of their arms. The only sound was the rhythmic swish of oil wells high up on the hills that overlooked the lake. Although partly hidden by trees, Angela felt the wells were an unnecessary blight on the local beauty. She said as much to Jim.

"Those wells make a fortune," he said. "They've pumped better than a thousand barrels a day for the past five years. And they don't make much noise. You can only hear them now because it's late and everything's quiet. They're modern wells and work on air pressure rather than gasoline motors."

"You sound like you like them."

He grinned. "My dad owns a twenty percent interest in all twelve of them. That car I drive came from money from those wells."

She let go of his hand and shoved him playfully in the side. "Here you're not even out of high school, and you've sold out to the money-hungry destroyers of our environment."

He grabbed her and pulled her close. "Who cares about this world? It's only here for our pleasure."

"What about our children? And our children's children?"

"I can't worry about them."

"You should," she said, feeling his warm breath on her face.

"Why? They might never be born."

He kissed her. He kissed the way he ate, and that wasn't bad. Deep and hard, but still with enjoyment. She felt herself sink into him; he pulled her tight against his body. He *was* like a redwood, strong and firm. His arms went around her, and his hands went down her back and over her butt. He was aggressive—Mary had told her. But she wasn't Mary, although last summer she wished many times she had been. She wasn't an expert in the art of making love. She had never even had a guy touch her below the waist. Jim moved his right hand to the front of her blouse and started to slip it down. God, it felt good, just his fingers getting close. But she pulled back.

"Don't I get a chance to come up for air?" she asked, trying to joke.

He reached for her. "I'll give you my air."

She held up her hand. "Hold on a sec. This is a little fast for me."

He smiled. He dropped his hands to his side and stared out at the water. "Do you want to go for a swim?" he asked.

"The water's too cold."

He started removing his shirt. "Hah! We're both hot. Besides, the night's warm. Come on."

"I don't have a bathing suit."

He pulled his shirt over his head, laughing. "That's the best part."

Angela felt dismayed. This was their first date, after all. Nothing like this had ever happened to her in Chicago. Jim unzipped his pants and began to pull them off. It didn't look as if he was wearing underwear.

"Wait," she said.

"What?"

"I can't swim," she lied.

"We don't have to go out deep."

"I have a cold."

"Angie."

"I'm just getting over one, really. I shouldn't go in the water."

He threw back his head and laughed at the moon. "I'm going swimming. You can join me if you want, or you can watch. But you'd better be careful if you watch, because I might suddenly jump out and pull you in. I've done it before, you know."

She giggled nervously. "I didn't know that."

Angela tried not to look while he pulled off his pants, but she ended up getting an eyeful. He had a nice—well, he was a nice boy, in all respects. Great buns.

Except he was kind of pushy, a side of him she had never seen before. It was funny how you really didn't know someone till you got intimate with them.

This is not intimacy. This is sexual insanity.

Jim ran naked into the water, splashing like a kid. At waist level he dived under, and she counted more heartbeats than she wanted before he reappeared, at least fifty yards farther out. He was a powerful swimmer. The light of the moon swam around him, and the ripples he sent out were like miniature silver waves.

"Come on!" he called.

"Next time!" she called back.

He swam to the center of the lake, a quarter of a mile out, and had her worried that he'd cramp up and drown. But then he rolled onto his back and leisurely began to paddle back in. She took off a shoe and touched the water with her foot. She shook her head. It must be fed with underground streams, she thought. The daytime temperature had averaged over eighty degrees for the last few months, and the water couldn't have been more than sixty degrees.

Jim must have a hardy constitution.

She saw an example of that hardy constitution a few minutes later when he reached the shore and came running out of the water toward her. She couldn't believe it. Until a few days ago her life was dull, and now she had a hunk, naked no less, chasing her in the middle of the night. She took one look at him and realized he had every intention of dragging her into the water, clothes and all. She ran off the grassy shore, across View Street, and into trees. She'd be damned if Jim wasn't still hot on her tail.

"I have a cold!" she shouted back to him.

"I don't believe you!" he answered.

Angela darted behind a clump of bushes, hoping to lose him, and bent down low to hide. She figured he'd be able to spot her in a second and had resigned herself to a drenching when she suddenly heard him cry out in pain. She stood up tentatively, figuring it might be a ruse. But she spotted him only fifty feet away kneeling beside a tree, holding his right arm. It looked as if he'd tripped and cut himself. Surprisingly, he had his pants on again.

He gets dressed and undressed faster than anybody I've ever seen.

She hurried to his side and helped him up.

"I guess I was in too much of a hurry to catch you," he said rather sheepishly.

"God," she whispered. His right arm was covered with blood. She couldn't even see where the cut was. "What happened?"

"I ran into a tree." He touched the tree they were standing beside. "This one."

"Does it hurt?"

"The tree? It did when it came running at me."

She giggled. "Silly. That's what you get for trying to drench me. Come on, let's go back to my place. I can dress it for you."

He was agreeable to the idea at first. But when they got to where he had deposited his shirt he wanted to wash the cut in the lake and bandage it with his shirt—tear it into strips, in other words. The wound was still bleeding, but Angela thought that was a bit extreme.

"Why don't you just put pressure on it?" she suggested. "That will stop the bleeding."

"Because it hurts. I don't want to touch it."

She nodded to the lake. "Is this water clean enough?"

"We drink it every day at school."

"So I've heard."

"What have you heard?" he asked.

"Never mind. OK, let's wash it." She reached down and picked up his shirt. "At least we'll be able to see how bad it is."

"I'm surprised how much it stings," Jim said. She suspected it was a nasty cut indeed. He hesitated before dipping it in the water. She knelt beside him and got her pants wet, too.

"Do you want me to help you?" she asked.

"Am I acting like a baby?"

"Not at all."

"Good," he said. "Can I kiss you again?"

"Yes. But first let's—"

He shut her up by leaning over and planting his lips on hers. He couldn't have been in that much pain. Once more he kissed her long and hard. Again she felt his hands on her body, tugging at the buttons on the front of her blouse. She tried to stop him, but he persisted, and she didn't really want him to stop anyway. Actually, she wanted him to strip her naked and make passionate love to her right on the spot. He leaned her head back on the grass and pulled her blouse open. She had a bra on, but that wouldn't be an obstacle to him for long. Not this guy.

This is a hell of a way to get to know each other. Then she felt a warm, sticky liquid being smeared across her belly as he squeezed her closer. It was totally silly of her, but for a moment she had forgotten he was bleeding. She sat up with a start, knocking him back.

"You're bleeding all over me!" she cried.

"It's OK."

"No. It's not OK." Her blouse was lying completely open; he had snapped free a couple of buttons in his eagerness to get to her breasts. The blouse was badly stained with blood, as was much of her belly and chest. She couldn't believe he had managed to bleed on her that much during just one kiss. She wondered how long it had lasted. "You've made a mess of both of us," she complained.

He laughed. "It'll wash off."

"I don't think so." She paused. "How's your arm?"

He held it up to the moonlight—seemingly without a care in the world—and she could see that it was soaked with blood, more even than a few minutes ago. "It doesn't look like it's going to fall off in the next minute," he said.

"Jim! You're really bleeding. You might have sliced a vein."

"That's why I wanted to tear up my shirt," he said.

"You just wanted to tear off my clothes."

He grabbed at her again. "Yeah."

She pushed him back. "We have to stop this bleeding."

He grinned wolfishly. "Why don't you kiss it and make it better?" He held it up to her face for her to do so. "Just a little peck."

She turned her head. "You're making me sick. Where's your shirt? I'm going to tie it on your arm—the whole thing. Let's not wash the wound in the water. It'll only encourage the bleeding."

"All right, Angie."

She knotted his shirt directly over the spot where she believed the cut to be. Jim gave a grunt but said nothing. She sat for a minute to see if the bleeding decreased. It appeared to do so. Her hands, all her clothes, were by this time covered with blood.

"It's getting better," she said, moving to get up. "Let's get back."

"In a minute."

"Jim."

He grabbed her and started kissing her again. Somebody had eaten his Wheaties that morning. But they were both so smeared with gook that the passion had lost all charm for Angela. Well, most of the charm. It still felt good to have his mouth on hers. He tasted great, like the steak he'd eaten for dinner. That rare steak.

Angie, dear, that might be the taste of his blood.

The thought was enough to cool her down. She finally managed to push him back and jump to her feet before he could kiss her again.

"We're going back," she said.

He glanced up at her and flashed a little-boy smile. "So soon?"

"Yes." She offered him her hand. "Before the sun comes up."

He kissed her once more as she said goodbye to him at his car. He wouldn't let her take him to a doctor because he said his arm was fine. He touched her right breast, under the bra, while he gave her the last kiss. She couldn't believe she let him. Mary said he was a monster, all right.

But a dreamy thought swam in Angela's mind as she let him touch her.

Maybe he's my kind of monster.

Angela eventually found herself in bed, alone under her covers. Supposedly alone, yet remarkably, she was with strange company in an alien world.

The World was alive. It had been for billions of years, ever since it could remember. Of course, nothing, no matter how alien, could remember death. For that reason the World believed it was immortal. Life would come to its surface, and it would kill it in that special way, and eat it, and give it everlasting life as it became part of itself. The World would go on and on, and nothing, it believed, could stop it.

The World was always hungry.

Especially for those who visited.

They were such easy prey.

Angela felt like a visitor as she walked through the flowered meadow. The sun was bright, yet somehow smaller than she remembered it should be. But that didn't matter. She had entered paradise and was happy. It had been a long journey, and now she could rest, free and unwatched.

Sweet aromas saturated the air. At a stream she knelt to refresh herself with a drink. But before she could sample the water she sat up with a start. For the sun had suddenly gone behind a dark cloud that had not been there a minute before. As it disappeared the meadow grew dark, but not in a normal way. The light changed to a sober red as the rays of the sun filtered through the strange cloud, floating in the sky above her head like some diseased heart.

"God," Angela whispered, peering up at the sky.

But God was not there. Not in this place, surely not.

Angela began to feel hot. A smell pushed its way into her nostrils. Not sweet or pleasant—but familiar. Yes, she knew what it was.

"No," Angela whispered. "No, God."

A bolt of lightning cracked the sky. It could have split it open, the underbelly of a massive airborne demon. But it was just a cloud that had burst, although it was no ordinary cloud. Now drops of blood fell as rain to earth.

But wasn't that the fatal joke? She wasn't on Earth, couldn't be. She had traveled far to enter paradise and had accidentally stumbled into hell.

The blood soaked her. Soon it was all she could smell, all she could see. A river ran red at her feet. But the blood didn't just fall from the sky onto the World. First it was sucked up from the ground.

Something mingled with the blood at her feet. This something was the brain cells of the World. The cells that gave the World thought, desire, cravings. The World had huge appetites that would never be filled. Such bittersweetness, this hunger, especially when it swam in the juices of previous harvests, around the raw flesh of the next unsuspecting victim.

A horrible pain started in Angela's feet. She screamed, hopping from foot to foot, trying to get away from the million invisible teeth that were trying to devour her. The pain, though, was much too great. She couldn't maintain her balance. She tripped, and in an instant the monster in the blood was over her body, on her face, even in her mouth, where it began to dine on the choicest of meats. . . .

Angela sat bolt upright in bed, her heart pounding, her nightgown soaked. Before she could catch her breath her guts lurched, and she had to run to the bathroom. She was barely in time to lose the contents of her stomach into the toilet. For a minute she sat dazed on the floor of the bathroom, drawing in deep, burning breaths that did little to warm the awful coldness in her limbs.

I'm getting the flu. It must be a killer.

Eventually she made her way back to bed. But she didn't go back to sleep right away. She didn't want to have that dream again. Never.

CHAPTER V

KEVIN WOKE HER THE NEXT MORNING BY BANGING ON her bedroom door. She moaned and rolled over. Her mouth was dry, and she could hear her heart pounding in her head. She knew it had to be Kevin. Her grandfather never disturbed her slumber. He was a great believer in sleeping late. Especially after a romantic evening.

"Go away," she called.

Kevin cracked open the door. "Are you decent?" he asked.

"I'm stark naked."

"Excellent." He opened the door all the way and peered in at her. "Are you OK?"

She closed her eyes. "I don't know. I might have the flu."

Kevin sniffed. "It smells like vomit in here."

"I threw up in the night."

"You should have thrown up in the toilet."

"It was dark. I might have missed." She re-opened her eyes. "What time is it?"

"Eleven."

"No way."

"Way, José."

"Christ," she said.

He sat on the bed beside her. "Where were you last night?"

"I was here and I was there." She sat up, keeping the sheet pulled up tight to her chin. He could have seen right through the nightgown she was wearing, and she didn't have a bra on. She spotted her clothes from the night before balled up in the corner. Kevin might have smelled the dried blood as well as her vomit. "Is it really eleven?" she asked.

"Yes." He put his hand to her forehead. "You don't have a fever."

"Good." She didn't have a headache either—not exactly, although her head felt strangely full, as if her brain had tried to expand during the night without her permission. She remembered her nightmare right then and shuddered. Where the hell had that come from?

"Do you have the chills?" he asked.

"No. I probably just ate something that didn't agree with me."

"What did you eat?"

"Two hot dogs." She hesitated. "I went to the game last night."

"By yourself?"

"Yeah."

"Why didn't you ask me?"

"You hate football."

"But I like cheerleaders," he said.

"You wouldn't have gone. We won."

He was surprised. "Against Balton?"

"We killed them. Forty-two to nine."

"Amazing. How did Jim Kline play?" he asked.

"What?"

"Jim. The quarterback, the one Mary thinks is the monster."

"He was awesome."

Kevin whistled. "He stank up the field last year. Maybe he has changed into something new."

Angela glanced out at the lake. Plastic was lying on the balcony staring at the water, as usual. The glare of the sun on the lake made Angela's eyes ache. "I better take a shower," she said. "And get dressed."

"Can I watch?" Kevin asked hopefully.

She smiled wearily. "When you're older."

Kevin left the room, and Angela showered. She joined him at the breakfast table not long after. She felt a bit better. Her appetite had definitely returned; in fact, she was starving. Her grandfather's door was closed, but he was already gone. He had left her a typed note on the kitchen table.

Angel,

Went to Chicago to watch the horses run off with my money. Take care of yourself. Try to do something your parents wouldn't approve of.

Your Old Man

"I hope when I'm seventy I'm still getting laid as often as he is," Kevin said when she had set the note aside. He had fetched the paper—it was spread over the kitchen table—and had helped himself to their bread and peanut butter.

"I hope when I'm seventy you'll still be interested in me," Angela said.

"By older did you mean *that* old?"

Angela chuckled. "Time will tell." She nodded to the paper. "What's new in the world?"

Kevin lost his easygoing expression. "You should know. You said you were there last night."

"What are you talking about?"

He turned the paper her way. There was a picture of a player from Balton High's football team on the front page. A handsome young man—his name was Fred Keith. The article was entitled MATADOR PLAYER CRIPPLED FROM THE NECK DOWN.

Angela cringed. "What? They had to help the guy off the field, but he didn't look bad. I can't believe this."

"He has a tube down his throat that's breathing for him." Kevin shook his head sadly. "He must have taken a hell of a hit."

Angela read the article.

Last night Fred Keith, a junior at Balton High, was rushed to the emergency ward of Balton Memorial after sustaining a neck injury in the fourth quarter of a football game between Balton High and Point High. Fred was playing right defensive guard and was injured on a play that scored Point's seventh touchdown of the night. Initially the injury was not thought to be serious. Fred was helped from the game by the team's trainer and an assistant coach. He wasn't even carried off the field on a stretcher—ordinary procedure when a cervical injury is suspected. The team's trainer, Steve Sperber, later said that he had seen the hit that had caused Fred's injury and hadn't thought it was particularly hard. "The kid barely banged him," Mr. Sperber was quoted as saying.

The kid was later identified as Larry Zurer, who said he hoped Fred felt better soon.

At the hospital it quickly became evident that Fred had sustained serious fractures to the third and fourth cervicals. Damage to that part of the neck often results in complete paralysis, and Fred has yet to regain feeling in any of his limbs. He tolerated the surgery on his neck well, however. But Fred is still having trouble breathing properly and has been hooked up to a respirator. The prognosis for complete recovery is considered poor, doctors say.

Fred's parents could not be reached for comment, although there is already talk of a lawsuit over the handling of Fred immediately after the injury was sustained. But it was the opinion of one doctor, who had seen the X-rays of the boy and who asked not to be

identified, that Fred would have been paralyzed from the neck down no matter how he
had been taken from the playing field. "That
boy's neck looked like it had been cracked by
a sledgehammer," the doctor remarked.

"Jesus," Angela mumbled as she set down the
paper.

"Too bad he's not around to heal the guy," Kevin
said. "Did you read that last comment from that
doctor?"

"I did."

Kevin raised a quizzical eyebrow. "I wonder
what Mary would have to say about that."

Angela continued to stare at Fred Keith's picture.
"I didn't tell you that Larry Zurer was another one
of the people Mary suspected might be a monster."

"That's an interesting coincidence."

"What are you saying?" Angela asked.

"Nothing. What are you saying?"

"I want to talk to Mary again."

"OK," Kevin said. "What for?"

"I just do." She scanned the kitchen. "But I want
to stop and get something to eat first."

"Why don't you just eat here?" Kevin asked.

Angela looked at the bread and the butter and the
fruit bowl and found herself repulsed. "I need
something more substantial," she said.

On the way to Balton they stopped at a McDonald's. She ordered a Big Mac and fries. Kevin found

her appetite fascinating, since she ordinarily ate like a bird. He would have been even more intrigued had he known that she felt like having another hamburger when she was through eating. What a flu, she thought. It worked in reverse.

Nguyen greeted her in his office. She had called to say she was coming in. The lieutenant asked Kevin to stay in the waiting room while he spoke to Angela. When his door was closed he asked her to have a seat.

"Why are you here?" he asked.

"I want to talk to Mary again."

"About?"

Angela shrugged. "What we discussed last time. Why she did it."

"I thought you said Mary refused to discuss anything about the shootings."

Angela could feel Nguyen studying her. He was smart, and her lies probably didn't fool him at all. "I want to try again," she said simply.

"Did you know that Mary might be getting out on bail soon?"

"No. I heard the opposite."

"Her parents have hired the top lawyer in the state," Nguyen said. "He's persistent. It's likely he'll be able to get her out on a technicality—the only way she'd ever get out."

"Will she go home?"

"I don't know. I'd advise against it, for her safety. I'd appreciate it if you could convince her to stay here."

"I doubt if I can do that."

"You can try."

"I'll try," Angela promised.

Angela was brought to the same boxlike room as before. Only now one of the overhead fluorescent lights had failed, making the place rather dark. Angela sat in the gloom wondering what she was going to say to Mary, about her date with Jim, about Fred Keith. She also thought about food. She was still starving. A steak for dinner sounded great, if she could last that long.

Nguyen brought Mary in this time. As before, she was handcuffed. When the lieutenant started to handcuff her to the chair on the other side of the gray table, Angela shook her head no. Nguyen was amiable. He nodded and left the room without a word.

Mary didn't look the better for her jail time. She had lost weight. The bandages she had on her head and hand looked like the same ones she'd had on the previous week. Her expression was guarded, and she appeared much more on edge than before.

"What have you found out?" Mary asked.

"About what?" Angela asked.

Mary snorted. "You wouldn't be back unless something out of the ordinary was bothering you."

"You don't put much stock in our friendship, do you?"

Mary ignored the comment. "Have you seen Jim?"

"Yeah."

Mary was instantly alert. She had radar like

nobody's business. "When and where did you see him?"

"Around. At school."

"Has he made a point of talking to you?" Mary asked.

"Yes. He told me you went crazy because he told you he didn't want to go out with you anymore."

Mary showed a thin smile. "Anything else?"

"No."

"Come on."

Angela sharpened her tone. "You come on. The last time I was here you gave me all this crap about you killing those two because they were aliens."

"I never said they were aliens. You said that."

"Monsters, whatever. Now I'm tired of it. You tell me the truth. Why did you come to that party with that shotgun?"

Mary regarded her closely. "What's happened, Angie? What's got you scared?"

Angela hesitated. "A boy broke his neck at the game last night."

Mary was interested. "Give me all the details."

"His name's Fred Keith. He plays for Balton—he used to play for Balton. Larry Zurer tackled him in the fourth quarter, and now Fred will probably be paralyzed from the neck down for the rest of his life."

Mary sucked in a breath. "I knew Larry was one of those bastards." She drummed her fingers on the tabletop. "What else?"

"When are you getting out?" Angela asked.

"I don't know. What else?"

"I hear you might be out tomorrow. You should stay here. I went to the funerals. Todd and Kathy's families are no fans of yours."

"Who cares?" Mary got up and began to pace. "If Larry's gone over, Carol's gone as well." She spoke to the wall. "How many more are there by now?"

"Are you figuring out how much ammunition you'll need?"

"Shut up," Mary snapped.

Angela jumped out of her chair. "You don't fool me one bit—your first hour out of here and you'll be after them."

Mary glared at her. "The minute I'm out of here *they'll* be after *me*. Look at yourself, Angie, and tell me who's fooling who. Is Jim suddenly head over heels in love with you? Did he tell you he had to dump me so that he could have you?"

Angela froze. "He did."

Mary pounded her knee with her good hand. "I knew it! What else? Are you going out with him?"

Angela's legs felt weak. She had to sit back down. "I went out with him last night."

Mary stared down at her. "Are you out of your goddamn mind?"

Angela peered up at her. "Most people think *you* are, Mary."

Mary stepped back around the table and plopped down in her chair. She chuckled bitterly. "My friend, Angela Warner. So hard up for male attention that she chooses one of the few human animals in the country to lust after."

"He chose me," Angela said.

"He chose you because he's worried about what I told you. Admit it, he asked you, didn't he? Maybe a few times?"

"Didn't you talk to her on Saturday?" "Didn't she tell you anything?" "Like what?" "What did she tell you?"

"They were normal questions," Angela said flatly.

"What did the happy couple do on their first date?"

"We ate together. In a restaurant. We didn't eat anybody."

"Then what did you do?" Mary asked.

"We went back to my place and screwed."

"I believe it. You're probably one of them by now."

Angela pounded the table. "Listen to me! What am I supposed to do? You tell me that Jim's walking death on the loose, and I'm just supposed to sit back and see if he kills somebody? You should be happy I went out with him. I'm carrying on your research."

Mary considered. "Did you sleep with him?"

"No."

"Did you kiss him?"

"Yes."

"Bitch," Mary said.

"You tried to kill Jim last week. I can't believe you're jealous that I went out with him."

Mary opened her mouth to snap at her friend

again but thought better of it. She briefly closed her eyes and took a couple of deep breaths. When she reopened them she reached across the table and took Angela's hand. Angela had thought Mary had bloodshot eyes the last time. Now they were more red than any other color.

"Jim is not in love with you," Mary said calmly. "He is not interested in forming a relationship with you. He wants to use you to get to me. He's worried about what you know. He will probably kill you eventually. He might do worse."

"He might turn me into someone like himself?" Angela asked.

"Yes."

"What is he, Mary?"

"I told you, I don't know."

"Did you know Point Lake was formed by a meteor millions of years ago?"

Mary scowled. "What does that have to do with anything?"

"I don't know."

"Why did you bring it up?" Mary asked.

"It's a concern of mine that I drink pure, healthy water."

"I'm serious!"

"It's hard to take you seriously, Mary. You tell me about a warehouse but can't remember where it's located. You talk about people disappearing inside this warehouse who are never reported missing. You tell me to watch out for Jim, that he's evil, even though he seems like such a fun-loving guy.

And every psychologist in the country is branding you a certifiable lunatic after what you did last week. Now I think it's time you gave me something concrete to go on, or else I'm going to have to conclude once and for all that you are what you appear to be: a young woman who committed murder in a jealous rage."

Mary sat back. She stared at the floor for a full minute and then sighed. "Chicken crates."

"Yes?"

"I hid behind crates that had held chickens while I watched them drag the two couples into the warehouse."

"And this warehouse is in Balton?" Angela asked.

"I think so."

"You think so? You were sure last week."

"Where Balton joins Kally," Mary said patiently. "It's hard to tell where one city ends and the other begins. The warehouse may have been in Kally. It was at the edge of town, I remember that much."

"How do you know the crates had contained chickens?"

"I could tell by the smell."

Angela stood. "Good."

"What are you going to do?"

"I'm going to find all the warehouses where chickens are stored in both Balton and Kally. Then I'm going to these places to search for an abandoned warehouse nearby. If I find such a warehouse, I'm going to break in and search for blood-stains on the floor."

"I told you I went back to the warehouse. They had been there already and washed away what was left of the blood."

"They couldn't have washed it all away. If it was there to begin with, I should be able to find traces of it." Angela stopped. "Or would you rather I didn't look?"

Mary was tough. "I'm curious why you're look-ing at all. What did you do after eating at the restaurant, Angie?"

"We went for a walk along the lake. We kissed."

"Don't rub my face in it. Is that all?"

"Jim cut his arm while he was chasing me," Angela said.

"Did he bleed?"

"A tremendous amount. Like a normal human being."

Mary frowned. "Blood," she whispered.

"It wasn't green or anything like that."

Mary snorted. "You still haven't answered my original question. Why are you here? Why didn't you just write me off as a basket case?"

"I told you what happened to Fred Keith."

"That wasn't what brought you back here. You're scared. What scared you? Jim?"

"No."

"What?"

Angela put her hand to her head. For a moment she felt dizzy; the room spun. She had that peculiar pounding in her head again, like when she woke up.

It had gone away when she had eaten. God, she was hungry again. She felt as if she could eat a cow whole.

"I had a dream," she said finally. "That's what scared me."

"What happened in this dream?"

Angela turned for the door. "I was eaten alive. That's all I remember. I'll talk to you later, Mary. Stay healthy."

"Stay alive, Angie," Mary said.

Nguyen hardly questioned Angela when she stopped by his office after talking to Mary. She fed him the same lies she had the previous week and doubted he believed her for a moment. She briefly wondered if he had been eavesdropping on their conversations, but decided it would have been against the law.

Kevin joined her in the waiting room and walked her out to her car.

"How did it go?" he asked.

"It's hard to say. We have to find a warehouse around here that stores chickens."

"Sounds like my kind of Saturday afternoon," Kevin said.

Of course Lieutenant Nguyen didn't believe Angela, because once more he'd both eavesdropped on and recorded the conversation she'd had with Mary. Officer Martin, one of the men who'd helped Nguyen capture Mary the night of the party, went into Nguyen's office carrying the tape. The two men listened to the conversation twice before speaking.

"We made a mistake searching for the warehouse in Balton alone," Nguyen said. "That may be why we didn't find it."

"It was my mistake," Officer Martin said. He was a short, squat man with a serious attitude toward life. His wife said they slept together with their guard dog. If Martin had a first name, he had forgotten it. Nguyen liked him. "Where's that other girl coming from?" Martin asked.

"Angela Warner? I don't know. Obviously she doesn't believe Mary's story—who would?—but there are elements in it that disturb her." Nguyen removed the tape from the player and fingered it uneasily. There was something about Angela's state of mind that was different from that of the previous week. Last Saturday Nguyen wouldn't have imagined Angela going out with Mary's boyfriend—a clear act of disloyalty. But perhaps Jim had some kind of power over girls. He was an extremely handsome kid.

Maybe he was more than that.

Jim reminded Nguyen of a young soldier he'd had under his command in Vietnam. The man's name had been Tran Quan; he was the best killer Nguyen had ever seen. On sorties into the jungle Tran Quan always killed more VC than the rest of his squad combined. He hunted like a snake, though, not like a human. He wouldn't stop at shooting or stabbing a victim in the back. Nguyen hated him and needed him at the same time.

But that need had been superseded the night he had found Tran Quan raping a village girl whom he had just shot in the head. He had smiled when he was caught in the beam of Nguyen's flashlight. Nguyen had killed him on the spot and never regretted it.

What did nice, clean-cut Jim Kline have in common with Tran Quan that Nguyen should link them together? He didn't know. But he was afraid what would happen if he didn't find out.

"I'd like to follow all three of these kids," Nguyen said finally. "Angela, Jim, and especially Mary. Would you help me?"

"Yes," Martin said. "I'd like to take Mary. It sounds like she won't be out on bail too long with that kind of attitude."

"She's seventeen, but you know how dangerous she is?"

"I saw proof at that party last week."

"Don't forget what you saw." Nguyen stood. "Let's look over our list of warehouses once more and concentrate on Kally. I'm sure Angela is doing the same thing right now. If there is a warehouse like the one Mary's described, I can probably pick up Angela's trail there."

Chapter VI

Angela and Kevin found a food wholesaler's warehouse listed in the local Yellow Pages. It had a Kally address, not a Balton one. Kevin said he knew where it was. It took them only twenty minutes to find. Of course, they were more interested in what was across the street from it.

Which just happened to be an abandoned warehouse.

It was right where Mary said it should be. Not far from a stack of smelly chicken crates. Angela parked beside them and climbed out. Since it was a Saturday, the industrial part of town was deserted. The smell of the nearby crates, though repulsive, just increased her hunger. She was going to have to ditch Kevin soon and go eat the contents of a supermarket. She pointed across the alley at the boarded-up back door of what had been a foam rubber warehouse.

"Could there be the blood of four dead bodies in there?" she asked hypothetically.

"Didn't Mary say the monsters wiped up all the mess?" Kevin asked.

Angela shrugged. "You know how sloppy monsters are. Let's go see what we can find. But let's get my nut wrench from the trunk. We can use it in place of a crowbar to yank the boards off."

"All right," Kevin said. "We may want to bring a flashlight, too."

Angela didn't like the look of the building, the feeling that surrounded it. Maybe it was haunted by ghosts that had not left the world happy. Or maybe that was another illusion.

"Yeah," she answered Kevin. "And try to get a shotgun."

They broke into the building with remarkable ease, leaving the door wide open behind them. They were quickly happy for the flashlight, though. The warehouse was huge. The door receded behind them to a tiny rectangle of light, their only connection to the real world. If she had thought the place creepy on the outside, inside she thought it was in dire need of an exorcism. Their steps echoed away from them like the footfalls of stalking phantoms. The air was stale. A faint smell of foam rubber permeated it, along with the odor of something she couldn't pinpoint. The rancid stench of decay, maybe?

"Is this a scary place or what?" she whispered.

"I wouldn't want to come here after dark," Kevin agreed. "I wonder if there's a light switch."

They searched but could find no switch. Angela suspected the electricity had been disconnected long ago, anyway. The owners were obviously not concerned about keeping up appearances in order to show the place to potential renters or buyers. A film of dust covered everything—the hard gray floor, the dark brown walls. But their search for the washed-away blood would have been hopeless if it hadn't been for the dust. For the absence of it, in one dark corner, drew the beam of their flashlight like a magnet. Only a few minutes inside the building and they were hurrying to the clean patch of concrete. It was remarkably circular, as if it had been drawn as an altar of sacrifice. Angela went down on her knees as Kevin held the light above her head. She touched the cold floor and peered closely.

"See anything?" Kevin asked.

She crawled forward, straining her eyes. And then, in a jagged crack that had probably been created by the settling building, she saw dried dark red stuff. She motioned Kevin to kneel beside her. They pressed the beam of the flashlight close to the crack. Kevin reached out and scraped some of the dark stuff with his nail.

"What is it?" Angela asked, her heart pounding.

"Looks like dried blood."

"Christ."

"I don't think it's his blood."

"Kevin."

"I know, this is bad. Good for Mary, maybe. Bad for the rest of the planet."

She stared at him. "Does this make you believe Mary's story?"

"I was joking," Kevin said. "I'm more inclined

to believe that Todd and Kathy and Jim killed four people here. That makes them monsters, certainly. But not the supernatural sort."

"Yeah." Angela took the flashlight and followed the crack farther. It stretched maybe fifteen feet across the dust-free circle, and it was choked with the dried blood. How much had they spilled, she wondered, that it covered so much of the floor? "Mary didn't see this when she came back," she said.

"If it had been real bloody to begin with," Kevin said, "she might not have gone down on her hands and knees when she came back. I guess you know what we have to do now?"

"What do you mean?" she asked.

"I think it's pretty obvious. We have to tell the police what we've found. It adds credibility to Mary's story."

"But Mary hasn't told the police her story."

"She might want to now," Kevin said. "A modified version of it."

"No."

"What do you mean—no?"

"I don't want to go to the police with this just yet."

"Why not?" he asked.

Angela looked back toward the lighted doorway, an easy two hundred yards away. She was having trouble breathing. The air had no life in it.

Did the people scream as they died, and did they suck all the life out of the air?

"I went out with Jim Kline last night," she said.

Kevin plopped down on the floor beside her. "Why?"

"He asked me. I said yes." She shrugged. "We went out after the game. We ate and then went for a walk along the lake."

He was hurt. "Why didn't you tell me?"

"I didn't want to hurt your feelings."

Kevin's face crumpled. In the harsh shadows cast by the flashlight it was particularly pathetic. "It hurts my feelings more that you'd lie to me about it."

"I'm sorry," she said. She wanted to touch him, to hold him, but couldn't in this hellish place. They had to get out into the air soon. She didn't know why she had chosen now to tell him about Jim.

"Do you like him?" Kevin asked.

"I don't know. Maybe."

Kevin snorted. "What about what Mary says? What about this dried blood? Are we just performing character research here? If we are, I'd say the guy gets a lousy rating."

"Kevin."

"What's wrong with me?" he asked.

That hurt—the worst of all questions. I love you. Why don't you love me? She honestly believed that she would have preferred to ask it than to answer it.

"There's nothing wrong with you, Kevin," she said as gently as she could. "There's something wrong with me."

"Yeah, right. A body overflowing with hormones."

She began to cry. It surprised her. The tears just sprang out. "I'm serious," she said. "I don't feel right."

Kevin quieted. He put his arm around her. "What's wrong with you?" he asked.

I'm hungry. I need another couple of Big Macs. I don't even care if they serve me the meat raw. I might even prefer it.

She sniffed. "I had a bad dream last night."

"Was I in it?"

She had to laugh, even though she continued to cry. "No. I was alone. I was far from home, in a horrible world. But I can't talk about that right now. And the reason I went out with Jim—I can't talk about that, either. I just want to tell you that I do care about you. You're my friend. That's all I can say right now."

Kevin took a moment to answer. "Are you going to see him again?"

"No," she lied.

"Will you promise me?"

She studied his lovely, innocent face. Those brown eyes that sparkled even in the darkness of the warehouse. She reached over and brushed his hair aside. She kissed his cheek.

Yes. I promise you that you are wonderful. That much I know.

"Yes," she said.

He continued to hold her eyes. He was sharp. Perhaps he believed her. Perhaps he didn't. But he did relax. "Why can't we go to the police?" he asked.

"I want to do more research first."

"On what?"

"Indians," she said.

"Huh?"

She let go of him and stood, wiping her hands on her pants, the flashlight tucked under her chin. "You said they lived here first. I want to hear their side of the story."

— CHAPTER VII —

ANGELA DROVE KEVIN HOME. THEY SPOKE LITTLE ON
the way. Kevin was still digesting the news that she
had gone out with another guy. Angela couldn't
stop thinking about food. She had nine bucks in her
purse, but she wondered if she needed to stop at an
automatic teller machine to get more money in
order to satisfy her hunger. She hadn't a clue what
was causing the immense craving. She couldn't be
pregnant, that she knew for sure.

Kevin was reluctant to leave her when she
stopped in front of his house. "Where are you
going?" he asked.

"To the library."

"Why don't you want me to come with you?" he
asked.

"Because I'm in a weird mood."

"You're always in a weird mood. I can help you."

Her stomach growled. It actually felt as if it were
digesting itself. "I have to go. Please? I'll call you
later."

Kevin got out slowly. "What are you doing
tonight?" he asked.

"I don't know. Resting. I think I do have the flu. I'll call you tomorrow."

"Fine." He shut the car door. "Stay away from the bad guys, A and W."

"I will."

She drove straight to the McDonald's, doing well over the speed limit all the way. She ordered another Big Mac and a Coke, leaving off the fries. It was a relief to put the food in her mouth and chew it. Yet the hamburger didn't satisfy her. They had cooked the meat too much, she thought. Nevertheless, she ordered another burger before she was done swallowing the first one. This time she told them she wanted it extra rare. The second one tasted better, and her hunger finally began to diminish, although it didn't go away completely. She contemplated ordering a third for the road, in case she got hungry later, but she couldn't eat three Big Macs! She had never eaten two before.

Next stop was the library. The old woman with the book tapes was behind the desk. She was listening to a Shakespearean play; it sounded like *Hamlet*. Angela wondered if she should explain to her that there were such things as headphones. The woman smiled kindly at her as she approached the desk.

"Can I help you?" she asked.

"Yes," Angela said. "I want all the material you have on two subjects. The Indians who lived in this area before the white man arrived, and the meteor that created Point Lake."

The old woman was excited. She looked like somebody's grandmother who had just gotten stoned on marijuana for the first time. "Do you like Indians?" she asked, turning off her tape. "I love them myself." She began to get up. "I know where every word on them is in this library. You just have a seat, and I'll bring you the material. What was the other thing you were interested in? Parking meters?"

Angela had to smile. "The meteor that formed the lake."

"I'll see what I've got," the woman said.

She was gone for some time. Angela worried that she had sat down and dozed off. But eventually she returned with a handful of material. Most of it was magazine articles and loose papers. There was one book, however—small and poorly bound. It looked as if it had been published at home with desktop equipment. Angela thanked the woman and went off in the corner to study. The woman put her tape back on—Hamlet was talking to his father's ghost.

There was only one article on the meteor and Point Lake. Angela read it first. The piece started with a discussion on how long ago the meteor—the article never debated for a moment whether it was a meteor or not—hit the Earth. Angela was surprised to learn the author had determined, using a carbon-14 radioactive decay test, that the meteor had hit the area as little as one hundred thousand years ago. Angela knew a little about astronomy. That wasn't very long ago. The author went on to describe the extremely high magnetic content of the rock in and around Point Lake. He finished by comparing it to another meteor site down in South America that was also now a lake. He said the two holes in the ground appeared to have been formed at the same time by the same highly magnetic ore from outer space.

He didn't say anything about the water in the lake being unhealthy.

Angela made a note of the author's name—Alan Spark. He was a professor of geology at the University of Michigan. That was only a ninety-minute drive from Point. Perhaps she'd visit him someday.

The material on the Native Americans took longer to wade through. Apparently the Manton had been the predominant tribe in the region until the white man had arrived a couple of hundred years ago and destroyed their life-style. There were numerous anecdotes of battles, of treaties signed, of more battles. It blew Angela's mind how many promises the U.S. government made and broke with the Manton. These Native Americans were either a trusting sort, or else they had short memories. Of course, they probably had no choice but to agree to the government's treaties. History was overrunning them, and there was no stopping it.

Buried in the history were several intriguing references to Point Lake. First off, its Indian name was *Sethia*, which meant Bath of Blood. Angela stopped and asked herself why they'd have given such a picturesque lake as Point such a terrible name. She couldn't imagine it and dug deeper for an explanation, figuring there must have been a major battle on its shores. But she could find no such reference. The name Sethia seemed to go way back, thousands of years perhaps. The word appeared loosely connected to another strange word —*KAtuu*. There was one story describing how the KAtuu emerged from the depths of the lake. Another spoke of the KAtuu coming out of the sky above the water. Try as she might, Angela couldn't find out exactly what the KAtuu were. In one place they were described as tiny insects too small for the human eye to see. In another they were spoken of as huge batlike beings that could cross great distances rapidly. In all ways they were described as deadly and to be feared. Above all, it was clear the Manton avoided Point Lake. It appeared that they successfully quarantined the area around the lake for decades at a time. It was a sacred rule among the Manton that no one of their tribe, under any circumstances, was to drink the water in the lake.

"Oh, my," Angela muttered to herself. "Somebody should have shown the local board of education these stories."

"Did you say something, dear?" the old librarian asked, turning off her book tape. Angela had been so engrossed in her research she didn't know what the woman was listening to now.

"I was just remarking to myself how fascinating the Indian history is in this area," Angela said.

The woman clapped her hands—she was pleased

to find a mutual fan. "Isn't it?" she asked. "But if you really want to hear wonderful stories about the Indians who lived around here, you must talk to Shining Feather. He can tell you stories firsthand. He's been around a long time."

"Pardon?"

"He's an old Indian who lives off Highway Seventeen near Wind Break. There's a shop there called Cheap Stuff. It's run by Shining Feather's great-great-granddaughter. You'll have to be careful with her. She'll try to sell you one of the rugs she makes whether you want it or not. I have three of her rugs at home in the closet."

"How old is this Shining Feather?" Angela asked.

"I don't know. He had white hair when I went to visit him for the first time." The old woman stopped and scratched her balding white head. She frowned. "That was back in the Depression, when I was a little girl."

Angela drove from the library to the shop, stopping along the way at a deli. Maybe she *was* pregnant and had conceived during an erotic dream. She bought the strangest thing to eat: a foot-long German sausage and a loaf of bread. She didn't even touch the bread, though. She gobbled down the sausage as she drove along Highway 17. It was only when she was done that she realized it hadn't even been cooked.

Still tasted great.

Cheap Stuff looked cheap from the outside. A

wooden shack built against an aging brick home, it was set back from the road and had a peeling wooden pony standing guard outside on a lawn of dust. Angela parked and went in. The great-great-granddaughter greeted her. It had to be the woman. She was Native American, and she had a blanket in her hands that she wanted to show Angela.

"I'm really here to see Shining Feather," Angela said, glancing about. The shop held shelves of pottery, woven baskets, hand-carved wooden figures—nothing that would interest a young woman raised in shopping malls.

"Feather, he's taking nap," the woman said. She was about thirty and very fat. She wore her black hair in a long, thick ponytail that reached past her waist. She shoved her blanket into Angela's arms. "This I give you for sixty bucks. It's a genuine Manton blanket."

The brown blanket looked as if it had been purchased at Wal-Mart and then had a couple of white pictographs sewn on it with thread. "I don't have sixty bucks," Angela said. "But I have a report on the Manton that I have to finish for class Monday. It's real important I speak to your great-great-grandfather. Could I come back at a later time?"

The woman was interested. "Are you saying good things about us?"

"Very good things."

"How much money do you have?"

"About two bucks."

The woman reached for a small clay figure on a nearby shelf. It was of a young native girl. "I'll sell you this and then go wake Feather."

"I don't want you to wake him. He might not like that."

The woman shrugged and put the figure in a brown bag. "He sleeps all the time. I'll have to wake him sooner or later so that he can get up to go to the bathroom."

Angela handed over her remaining two dollars, and the woman disappeared into the back. Angela decided she definitely had to stop at an ATM on the way home. She wasn't going back to her grandfather's place without groceries. She checked the time—five thirty-two. Jim had said he wanted to see her again at seven.

The woman reappeared and gestured that Angela was to follow her into the house portion of the structure, which was a questionable improvement over the retail part. They went through a messy kitchen and an impoverished living room into a tiny bedroom. Here things were neater; the bed was made, and the window was open, facing the sunset. The room smelled nice; a stick of incense burned in the corner. Shining Feather sat wrapped in a blanket in front of a fuzzy TV. He didn't look as if he'd been asleep at all. He glanced over as Angela entered and said something she did not understand.

"What?" she mumbled.

"He said, 'Hi, how are you?'" the woman said.

"He doesn't speak English?" she asked.

"He used to, but he's forgotten most of it. He prefers Manton. I will translate for you." She pointed. "Sit there in front of him, on that blanket. You like that blanket? I got it at Wal-Mart, on sale."

"It's very fine," Angela said, taking her place on the floor at the old man's feet. He was small and bent; the threads of white hair on his head were few and far between. But his skin was not excessively wrinkled for someone of his great age, and his black eyes, as they peered down at her, were keen and alert. It was almost as if he saw things about her she'd rather he couldn't see.

What have I got to hide?

Things. A strange story of monsters. An illicit kiss. A warehouse stained with blood. A huge appetite. She was keeping a few secrets these days.

"Hello," she said to the old man.

He nodded. He might have understood some English even if he didn't speak it. He said something to the woman in Manton.

"Feather wants you to mention in your report that the Manton were the greatest warriors that ever lived," the woman said.

Angela smiled back at Shining Feather. "Tell him that I have already done that." The woman translated her words before Angela continued. "Tell him that I would like to ask him some questions about Point Lake."

Once more the woman relayed the message. Angela was surprised when Shining Feather forcibly shook his head. "He doesn't want to talk about the lake," the woman said. "He says it's a bad place."

"That's specifically what I wanted to talk to him about," Angela said.

Shining Feather continued to speak. "He says he was the one who convinced some white settlers not to drink the water from the lake," the woman translated. "He says they didn't listen to him at first, but they learned to listen. He says that all the water drunk in the area comes from wells, not the lake, and he is responsible for that."

Angela shook her head. "Tell him that the water for the new school that was built on the lake comes from the lake, and that several kids have gotten sick at the school, and that we don't know what the sickness is."

After the woman relayed the message, Shining Feather grew agitated. He pulled his blanket tighter and squirmed in his seat. He began to speak more rapidly than before. "He says the sickness is from the water in the lake," the woman said, "and that children must not drink the water. He says if they stop immediately they will get better, but if they don't stop, terrible things will happen to them. He says you must go to the people in charge of the school and alert them to the danger. He says this happened before to white settlers. Many of them got sick until they listened to him. But he says all those settlers got better just by staying away from the water."

"Ask him what things will happen if people continue to drink the water," Angela said.

The old man shook his head when the question was relayed. "He will not speak of it," the woman said.

"Why not?" Angela asked.

The old man kept shaking his head. "He says you don't want to know what will happen," the woman said.

"Ask him why the lake was named Sethia by the Manton," Angela said.

Shining Feather responded. "He says you don't want to know," the woman said.

"Tell him I know the name means the Bath of Blood," Angela said.

Shining Feather became silent for a moment, staring at her. Finally he spoke softly to his great-great-granddaughter. "He wants to know what else you know," the woman said.

"Tell him I have read about the KAtuu, and that I—"

Shining Feather interrupted her with a yell. He shook his head vigorously and began to speak in Manton. "You are not to say that word," the woman said. "He says it is an evil word from an evil time. But he wants to know why you want to know about that word."

Angela looked the old man in the eye. "Tell him that several of the kids at the school may have changed in some way, and I am wondering if they have changed into—KAtuu."

Shining Feather was obviously disgusted that she had said the cursed word again because he did not immediately respond. When he did his voice was once more soft. "He wants to know in what way the children have changed," the woman said. "He wants to know if anyone has died, and he wants to know how they died." She added, "This is weird."

"Two people have died," Angela said. "They were killed by a girl who was convinced the people had changed into something evil. But the people, before they died, might have killed others." Angela paused. "They might have eaten four people alive."

Shining Feather was distressed by her answer. He continued to watch her, his eyes more alert than before, less kind. He spoke again. "He wants to know if the girl was able to kill all the strange children," the woman said.

"No," Angela said.

Shining Feather spoke. "How many are still alive?" the woman asked.

"I don't know," Angela said. "Why did the Manton call the lake the Bath of Blood?"

Shining Feather answered. "Because it was where the drinking of blood always started," the woman said.

"I don't understand," Angela said. "The lake was filled with blood?"

Shining Feather responded. "The lake is filled with water," the woman said. "The—he doesn't want to say the word—are filled with blood."

"I'm confused," Angela said. "Are the KAtuu

normal people who have changed as a result of drinking the water in the lake?"

Shining Feather scowled at the word. It really annoyed him. Angela didn't know how to get around using it. He responded. "He says that nothing about the 'changed ones' is normal," the woman said. "He says they change all at once, but very slowly, too."

"What does that mean?" Angela asked. "He's contradicting himself."

Shining Feather spoke. "He says they change on the inside before they change on the outside," the woman said. "They are hard to recognize at first."

"How can you recognize them?" Angela asked.

Shining Feather's eyes bored into her as he spoke. "They are always hungry for blood," the woman said.

No, I don't want blood. I just want hamburgers and sausage. I don't want blood!

"Oh, no," Angela whispered.

Shining Feather suddenly leaned over and grabbed Angela's wrist. She tried to shake off his hold, but he was strong. He tightened his grip and felt along the soft tissue just below her thumb. He was feeling for her pulse. She went still and let him complete his examination. He didn't like what he found. A few seconds later he threw her hand aside and pointed angrily toward the door, yelling something in Manton at her.

"He wants you to get out," the woman said, getting up in a hurry. She took Angela by the arm and pulled her to her feet. "He wants you to get out now and never come back. You've upset him."

"But I have to talk to him some more," Angela protested. The woman wouldn't let go of her. Angela was literally being dragged out the door, but she was able to shake free and took a step back toward the old man, who continued to watch her as if she had the plague. "What's wrong with me?" she demanded. "Why are you treating me this way?"

She couldn't believe his response, especially after the way he had carried on about the word. "KAtuu," he said.

"You must leave now," the woman ordered.

"I am not KAtuu!" Angela screamed. "I am a teenage girl. Why do you accuse me of that when I come to you for help?"

"Get out of here," the woman said, grabbing at her hand again.

"Leave me alone," Angela yelled, shaking her off. She took another step toward Shining Feather. Even though he saw her as evil, he was not afraid of her. "Why do you call me KAtuu?" she demanded. "I've hurt no one."

"What want?" the old man asked, and though it was broken English, his question was clear.

"I want to know if this thing is real," Angela said. "And if it is real, I want to know how to stop it before it spreads."

Shining Feather reached up and removed a small gold chain from around his neck. He held it out to her. At the end of the chain was a tiny golden amulet of a hanging bat, which had been hidden beneath his shirt. Angela took it and studied it closely. The bat was missing its head.

Shining Feather nodded. "K Atuu."

Angela frowned. "What happened to its head?"

"Wear," he said.

"Around my neck? But what good will that do?" She was desperate. "What am I supposed to do?"

The man made a slashing motion at his neck. "Kill them," he said.

"Who?"

"The hungry ones," he said.

"I have to cut off their heads?" she asked.

"Kill them," he repeated.

"What about me?" she asked. "Am I infected, too?"

He glanced out the window in the direction of the setting sun. The bloated orange globe was already halfway over the side of the Earth, falling into nighttime. The room had begun to darken, to grow chilly. Angela felt a shiver go through the length of her body as the old man turned his eyes back on her.

"Hungry?" he asked.

She nodded weakly. She was starving right now. "All the time."

"The water. The blood." He shook his head sadly and muttered something in Manton. Angela gestured to the woman.

"What did he say?" Angela asked.

"You swam too deep," the woman said.

"But I have never swum in the lake. It's too cold."

Shining Feather lowered his head and spoke in Manton.

"What?" Angela said.

"Your blood is as cold as the lake," the woman translated.

Angela could feel her heart pounding. But what flowed through her veins she no longer knew. "I think I will leave," she said.

The woman was spooked. "I think you had better."

Chapter VIII

On the way home Angela found a grocery store that took personal checks so she didn't have to locate an ATM. She bought all kinds of food, it was true, but who was she fooling? She purchased more red meat than she and her grandfather ordinarily ate in a month. Big steaks, fat steaks. She asked the man in the meat department if he had any cattle in the back, and he didn't laugh because she wasn't laughing when she asked him. She almost cried when the cashier asked if she was expecting company.

"Yes," Angela said. "They're from out of town."

Plastic was waiting for her at the front door when she got home. She was whining. Angela had forgotten to feed her that morning. Angela searched for a can of dog food but couldn't find any. She ended up tossing Plastic a raw steak on her upstairs balcony that overlooked the lake. The dog chewed away happily.

Angela was cooking herself a steak when the front door opened and in walked Jim Kline, star quarterback, heavy water drinker, Batman himself.

He still had his head on his shoulders. He looked up at her in the kitchen, a level above, and nodded. It was dark, and the only light she had on was a small lamp on a table in the living room beside where he stood. It didn't seem to bother him. Her steak sizzled on the hot pan.

"Hello, Angie," he said. "Am I early?"

"No. Come in. I was just making dinner. Are you hungry?"

"I'm starving," he said.

So, my darling boy. Are you a monster? Do you eat people? Do you want to eat me? Do I have to kill you? Are you from another planet? Are you evil? What do you want to do tonight? Kiss me? Love me? Make me more like yourself? Ah, my darling boy. Isn't that why you asked me out? Isn't that why you came to this world? To consume all the pretty young babes? And make them more evil than they already are.

"Should we eat here?" Angela asked when she had two steaks sizzling in the black pan. Jim sat silently at the kitchen table, watching her in the dark.

"At the oil wells," he said.

"You want to hike up there?"

"Yes."

"Fine." She knew why she hadn't gone for her grandfather's shotgun. First of all, he didn't have one. Second, there was a part of her that was in love with the dark side. There always had been, really— it was probably the same in all people. Jim both repelled and attracted her. His manner was cold. He was making no pretense of loving her tonight. He probably realized it was unnecessary. The baptism—whatever he had done to her—was complete, and she was already damned—at least from his point of view. There were also the things Mary had told her about him. Angela still couldn't say she believed Mary, but she didn't disbelieve her, either. That was saying a lot. If Jim wasn't a monster, he was far from being a normal jock.

"I want to eat and look down at the lake," he said.

"It sounds romantic," she replied. She wasn't being sarcastic because she truly was looking forward to being with him in the worst way. It was as if her mind were operating on two levels. He was bad, but he was so bad he looked *good.* She was dying for him to kiss her, to touch her. She craved his fingers on her as much as she craved juicy steaks. But he wasn't horny for her—he just sat there staring at her.

"You look pretty tonight," he said.

"Thank you," she said. She hadn't meant for him to come. She had planned to keep her promise to Kevin, to herself, intending to call him to say she wasn't feeling well. But she had gotten home late and had had to make herself something to eat—and then he had just walked in. . . .

"What did you do today?" Jim asked.

"Nothing."

"Did you see Mary?"

"Yes."

"What did she say?"

"Nothing," she said. Then there was the feeling that she needed him. Her body was changing. A doctor wouldn't understand how. But Jim knew; she could see subtle signs of change in him, too. His right hand rested on the kitchen table. His fingernails—as if they had been caught in something heavy—were all black. He tapped them lightly on the wooden tabletop and sent rhythmic echoes through the silent house.

"Is the steak almost done?" he asked.

"I just put it on."

"It doesn't matter."

"I guess not." She turned off the flame. "Let's go. I'll put the food in a sack."

But everything she thought about Jim and her reaction to him was also absurd. She hadn't yet forgotten that she was a human being. She certainly wasn't ready to kill anybody. She would die before she did that. In the bathroom, before leaving the house, she put Shining Feather's amulet on under her shirt. She didn't know what protection it could afford her. Maybe none. But she kept it close to her skin nevertheless. It reminded her of the old man's command:

Kill them—the hungry ones.

Jim didn't say a word as they hiked up to the oil wells, and she didn't mind. It was all she could do to catch her breath as she tried to keep up with him. He carried the sack of food, though; the smell of it pulled her like a leash on a puppy. She had tossed a loaf of bread and a bottle of wine in with the steaks.

The wells were tall, insectlike structures. There were only six that she could see, not the twelve he had mentioned. They plowed the earth with tireless indifference, sucking it dry of its natural resources. Yet in the light of the moon they were sensual. The silver light gleamed on the oily tubing. Up and down, in and out—pumping. Her thoughts reeled in lustful circles. If Jim had tried to undress her at that moment, she would have wished for scissors to help him.

They sat at the concrete footing of one of the wells, the valley and lake stretched splendidly out beneath them. They reached for their food. Jim ate and drank some of everything, but Angela just wanted her steak—extra rare, if it could be called that. She ate with her hands, and that made it taste all the better.

"The lake is round," Jim said when they were done eating. He was right, of course—the water appeared a perfect circle when seen from above. From space, in the moonlight, it probably appeared to be a single pale eye. A cloud could cross the sky and make the eye blink. Angela considered telling Jim her nightmare, but dismissed the idea. She didn't know what he knew of her suspicions. Better to keep it that way.

In case she had to kill him after she loved him.

But she was no Mary. She still couldn't imagine killing anybody.

"I hear it was formed by a meteor," she said.

"It was. A hundred thousand years ago."

She turned to him. "How did you know that?"

He shrugged. "It's known. Can you imagine it? A hunk of rock comes hurtling out of the sky and crashes here. In a fraction of a second the impact liberates more energy than a thousand nuclear warheads. This valley is formed, and for days on end it is a valley of fire. Of molten iron rock melting deeper and deeper into the earth, becoming a part of it. Cooling finally, and leaving a bowl for the water to gather in."

"Sethia," she said. His description evoked powerful images. It was almost as if he had been there to witness the coming of the meteor.

He frowned. "I don't know that name."

"That's what the Manton called Point Lake."

"What does it mean?"

"I don't know," she said. "How's your arm?" He had on a long-sleeved shirt. She couldn't remember if he had cut the right or left arm. She wondered if he could.

"It's better," he said.

"Is it bandaged?"

"Yes."

"Does it hurt?" she asked.

"No." He stood suddenly. "Let's go."

"Where?"

"Swimming."

"Should you go swimming with your cut?"

"I don't care," he said.

She felt fear. "The water's cold."

He stuck out his arm. "You'll be hot by the time you walk back down."

She was sweating by the time they reached her house. She didn't know what was going to happen next. The fact was, a potential KAtuu was asking her to go swimming in a Bath of Blood. Of course, people swam in the lake all summer, and none of them ate their neighbors. She wondered if it was possible that she would look back on these days when she was thirty years old and wonder if she hadn't been taking drugs. She certainly had thrown logic to the wind. She was close to believing in monsters, and at the same time she wanted to sleep with one.

Jim kissed her the moment they stepped inside her house.

He kept on kissing her.

It was better than the previous night. *He* was better. He was a hunk of male meat wrapped around the deepest nerve in her body. It was cool, she thought. He could eat her when he was done. As long as she got to watch. He ran his hands over the front of her blouse, and she moaned with pleasure and pain, never realizing before how close the two could be. She wanted him so bad it hurt.

He led her deeper into the house. Up to her bedroom. But they didn't stop there—more's the pity, she thought. He opened the door onto the balcony. Plastic looked up from her white steak bone and dashed inside the house. Jim stepped out and surveyed the calm lake. The air was even warmer than it had been the night before, silent as a tomb.

"Let's swim," he said.

Don't you want to exercise another way?

"How deep is this lake?" she asked aloud.

"Deeper than you imagine." He pulled off his shirt. He was built like Hercules. His right arm was bandaged. He flashed a faint smile—his first smile of the evening—when he saw her eyes dart to the white gauze. "Do you still have your cold?" he asked.

She hesitated. "No."

He began to take off his pants. "Can you swim?"

"I can swim," she said. She thought about the amulet around her neck. She didn't want him to see it. "But I have to go to the bathroom first."

"Go." He was practically naked.

She ran inside to the bathroom and pulled off the gold bat with no head. She couldn't imagine what it symbolized; the KAtuu surely were not bats. They were supposed to be alien monsters. She stuffed it in the medicine cabinet.

She heard a loud splash. He had already dived in. This was her chance. She could run out to her car and drive away. She could go over to Kevin's house and huddle in front of his TV and watch a rented horror movie and eat popcorn and have a nice normal safe Saturday night. But something kept her where she was, and she had another insight into what it was. She was horny as hell, sure, and who really believed in monsters? But if there was an evil force at work there, then she couldn't simply run away and pretend it didn't exist.

"What am I supposed to do? You tell me that Jim's walking death on the loose and I'm just supposed to sit back and see if he kills somebody? You should be happy I went out with him. I'm carrying on your research."

She had yelled that at Mary spontaneously, but it must have come from deep inside. She had to get close to Jim to see what he was. It was the only way she'd be able to make up her mind what to do.

Angela did not reach for a bathing suit as she walked back to the balcony. It was research, after all.

Jim was a hundred feet out. He waved as she stepped out into the moonlight. "Come on," he called.

Sethia. Bath of Blood. KAtuu. Cold as the lake.

"Coming," Angela whispered. She slipped out of her clothes and let them fall on the boards. The night air touched her where she was seldom seen. She crept to the edge and peered down. The water glittered like a million-faceted diamond. She did not know how deep it was at the edge. She didn't want to break her neck and end up paralyzed like poor Fred Keith.

"Hurry," Jim shouted.

"OK," she said, mostly to herself. It would be OK.

She jumped in.

The shock was so complete she didn't register it

at first. Her feet sank down without touching the bottom. She kicked up vigorously and broke the surface. Then the cold hit her; she could have landed on an iceberg.

"Ah!" she yelled.

Far out in the ice pool Jim snorted. "Swim!" he called. "It will warm you up."

He was wrong about that. The farther she swam from shore, the colder she got. She suspected she was losing body heat faster than any form of exercise would generate it. There was no way she could stay in more than a minute.

But then Jim met her and pulled her toward him and kissed her again. She could feel his body against hers and realized Mr. Shining Feather was wrong about this guy and how cold he was. Too hot to be cold was all she could think as his mouth pressed against hers. A powerful warmth flowed beneath her shivering flesh, sucking the blood deep into nerve endings she never imagined lived inside her body. She tilted her head back and went limp in his arms, letting him hold her afloat as his tongue slid over her throat. Straight overhead she could see the moon, cut in two by the shadow of space, and she felt somehow cut in pieces because try as she might she couldn't squeeze him close enough to quench her longing for him. He was one huge steak as rare as God made them, and she was lucky above all the girls on the planet to find him.

"Sweet," she whispered aloud.

Jim suddenly snapped her head back onto his mouth, and her ecstasy deepened beyond recovery even with the sharp pain that stabbed into her mouth. She had bit her tongue, or maybe he had done it. But the taste of blood in her mouth was the taste of pleasure. The pounding in her head that had plagued her all day returned a thousandfold, but now she fed it with a juice she had never dreamed of. It seemed to come out of Jim and into her mouth, where blood swam around their tongues like a forbidden elixir swirled in a sacred chalice. Yet there was so much of it that she couldn't imagine that it all belonged to her. But that was the heart of this seduction. Nothing belonged to anybody. Throw your body and soul into the temptation; let it all come back in tremors of satisfaction. Kissing him was such joy that the pounding in her brain was drowned by the sensation, swept away on a wet wind that blew from out of time, a wind that washed away her last thread of innocence and left her naked in the center of the cold lake.

How long he held her she wasn't sure. It seemed an eon had elapsed when he finally led her by her hand out of the water and up onto her balcony. Her skin was white marble; the drops of water that clung to it were like shards of ice. Yet she no longer shivered. She wasn't even sure if she still breathed.

They went into her bedroom and lay on the sheets beside each other. He looked at her, and she stared at him. His eyes were deep and wide; she could see space inside them that belonged to another dimension. They were also her own eyes—newborn twins—seen in unnatural reflection. She watched her own alien landscape unfolding in them even as she closed her eyes and fell into darkness.

She was in the mind of the immortal World, but she was not on the World. Her body was being sent away to feed. Her body, not her soul. She didn't have or need one of the latter. She had the mind of the World, and the World was always hungry. As she flew through the black abyss she dreamed of satisfying her cravings on the flesh of those who had been called brother and sister, but who were now enemies, only to be destroyed.

After some time she felt the wind on her face. The sun, a huge ball of fire in the sky, stung her eyes. Everything seemed strange to her, and yet she knew this place. Her body had grown up here. This was the Earth, and this had been home before she had been consumed by the World. She felt no nostalgia upon returning, only her need to feed.

In the distance she saw human beings approach. She smiled and waved at them as she stepped away from the vehicle that had brought her to Earth. She spoke to them. They were happy to see her again. They thought she was the one who had left the Earth months earlier to explore the World. They didn't know that the whole time she spoke to them she thought only of how they would taste. Later, in the dark, she would know.

The sun was too bright. It made her feel weak.

She was anxious to get inside and sleep.

And dream.

She dreamed many dreams. That was all there

was in the mind of the World. Nightmare upon nightmare. There was no need to awake, it constantly whispered.

But her body eventually awoke and went forward with a vengeance.

Time passed. Nights of feeding. Days of deception. Nights of stalking. Then, in the end, days of hiding, of fleeing. Because in time all the close friends of the body she inhabited were dead and eaten, or else they were like herself, running from those who had begun to suspect that the far-off World was not a place to build a second home, but a place to die a death that never ended.

In the end hiding became much more difficult because as time passed the body changed into a thing that brought terror to those who laid eyes upon it. Yet this new body was superior in many ways. It was stronger; it could fly. She could feed in one spot and be many miles away a short time later. But she had also changed in a manner different from anything that walked the Earth. She could no longer disguise herself or her true purpose. Feeding became difficult, then next to impossible. She began to weaken. The sun became intolerable, and she shunned it in the depths of the Earth. But that was a mistake, for she boxed herself in. With a group of those she had transformed she was cornered in a black cave. Humans in red uniforms broke in. Hand-held weapons that fired beams of burning ruby light flashed before her eyes. One of her kind was hauled into the circle of weapons and decapitated by a beam that cut down everything in its path. Then another of her kind was killed, and still another, until she was all that remained. The humans gathered around her, and there was triumph in their eyes. But she did not beg for mercy. She was a part of the World. It would live forever. More humans would travel from the third planet to the fifth, and more of her kind would take birth. The seeds of the World would spread. In the end its hunger would be satisfied.

Which was her last thought as her head was sliced from her body.

Angela awoke and opened her eyes. She lay all alone on top of her bed. She was freezing cold and had to pull the blankets over her. As she did so she saw Jim sitting naked on the balcony, staring out at the dark water of the lake.

"Jim," she called. "Come back to bed."

He ignored her. His body was so ghostly in the light of the moon it could have been made of imagination. She'd talk to him a minute. Now she was hungry. Getting up, she crept into the kitchen.

The clock read exactly twelve midnight, but the second hand did not move as she watched it. Broken, she thought—it felt much later than midnight. She opened the icebox and took out two steaks. They sizzled in the pan as she turned up the flame of the stove, but she didn't let them cook long. She just wanted to take the chill off, make them taste as if they had been alive not long before.

She ate both steaks without asking Jim if he wanted one.

He could get his own food, she thought.

Later, when she returned to the bedroom, Jim was no longer on the balcony, or anywhere else. She stepped out into the night and peered at the water, watching the ripples rock back and forth. They were strong in the immediate area; it was as if someone had just dived in.

"Jim?" she called.

She had heard no splash.

"Jim?"

And as she waited nobody surfaced.

"Sethia," she whispered. The word filled her with dread yet seemed to bring her back to her senses. She turned and walked back into the house. In the bathroom she took the amulet Shining Feather had given her and placed it around her neck. Almost immediately she remembered her nightmare and her long, cold swim with Jim. Her tongue ached in her mouth. He had bitten her. Or had she bitten both of them? She could not be sure.

Once more, as it had the previous night, her stomach lurched, and she thought she'd vomit up the meat she had just eaten. But the steaks stayed down, and soon she was able to get back into bed and cover herself. She fell asleep holding on to the decapitated bat. Horrible as the gold carving was, it seemed to keep away the bad dreams.

CHAPTER IX

CLASSES WERE NOT IN SESSION AT THE UNIVERSITY OF Michigan on Sunday. Angela didn't expect them to be. But she drove the two hours to the college with the hope that she'd at least be able to find one person who could tell her how to get hold of Professor Alan Spark, the author of the article she had read on the meteor. Luck was with her. She spoke to only one janitor and two students in the science building and was directed straight to the professor himself. It seemed Spark reserved private tutorial hours on the weekends for his students.

He was unoccupied when she entered his office. A tall, thin man of about forty, he had a trimmed brown mustache and the nervous movements of a bona fide bookworm. Judging by the photographs hanging on his walls, which showed him in various exotic parts of the world, he led an interesting life. He welcomed her and asked her to have a seat. At first he thought she was one of his students. She quickly explained that she was a senior at Point High and that she was doing an article for *The*

Point Herald on the safety of the water she and her classmates were drinking. He asked where she had heard of him, and she showed him the article from the science journal, which she had stolen from the library. He was immediately interested.

"I can give you my point of view on the matter," he said. "But I'll have to ask that you keep my name out of your article."

"Why's that?" she asked.

He gave a wry smile. "Because I want to continue to teach at this fine institution of higher learning, and—according to my superiors and my wife—I've created enough controversy in regard to the water in Point Lake. Of course, you remember the illnesses reported among the students at your high school last fall. I assume that's why you're doing your article."

"I didn't live in Point then, but I've read about them."

"Over thirty students reported various symptoms: nausea, headaches, blurred vision. There were several episodes of fainting. Experts were called in to study the matter: physicians and chemists and the like. I wasn't invited, however, because I was not a favorite of the local school board."

"Why didn't they like you?" Angela asked.

"I had already spoken out against placing the school next to the lake well before it was built. I was specifically worried about having the school's drinking water come from the lake. I didn't believe it was healthy to drink."

"Why?" she asked.

"This is where I ran into difficulty with the school board and their assembled experts. I am a geologist. I am not a physician or a biologist or a chemist. My specialty was not viewed as relevant to the matter of the drinking water, although I had done extensive studies on the lake and the local terrain. My specific views, when I finally aired them, were seen as irrelevant. In fact, I could go so far as to say I seriously damaged my reputation as a scientist in general by speaking against the location of the school."

"What did you think was wrong with the water?" she asked. He was slow getting to the point, and she was already hungry, although she had eaten in the car before going to look for him. She had eaten pretty much nonstop since she had awakened that morning. It was the only thing that soothed the throbbing inside her head. It was ten times worse than it had been the day before. What the hell had Jim done to her last night? she wondered. Besides bite off a chunk of her tongue. Her mouth continued to ache.

"You have read my article on the meteor that formed Point Lake," Spark said. "In it I talk about the high magnetic content of the iron ore that was thrown off when the meteor struck the Earth. The effect of that magnetism is strong at the location of the school. It is extremely strong on the bedrock of the lake." He paused. "Have you ever read about the health problems of people who live next to high-tension electrical wires?"

"No," Angela said.

"They often complain of headaches and fatigue. Not all people, you understand, just some. There are various theories as to why this is so. A popular one is that the electromagnetic balance of the body is upset by the magnetic field the wires give off."

"Wires give off magnetic fields?" she asked. He was too much the scientist—he was losing her.

"Yes," he said. "A magnetic field is generated in a circular direction around electrical current of a wire. That's simple physics. Now, at Point Lake we have a situation where a large body of water is resting on top of highly magnetic iron ore bedrock. When the plans for the school were being drawn up I raised the point that I thought it *might* be unhealthy for the students to drink water that had been subjected to a magnetic field on a continuous basis."

"Can water become magnetized?" she asked.

"This is one place where I ran into trouble with the school board and the scientific community as a whole. To answer your question—in the traditional sense, no. You cannot have magnetic water. You need a material such as iron to create a positive and magnetic polarity. By the way, do you know how many polarized atoms are required for an entire iron body to become magnetized?"

"I can't say that I do," Angela replied.

"Less than one in a hundred," Spark said.

"Really?" Angela nodded as if she was impressed. What he was saying *was* interesting, but she wasn't sure where he was going with it. Her stomach growled. Feed me or I will eat you, it seemed to be saying to her.

"It is a phase transition," Spark continued. "One moment an iron ore is nonmagnetic, and then just a few more atoms are polarized and the whole body of matter becomes magnetic. It's a fascinating phenomenon. Anyway, where was I? Oh, yes. I spoke against the students drinking water that had been exposed to such a magnetic field. Even though water itself cannot be made magnetic, there are subtle changes that take place in water that has been exposed to such a field. Water is made up of two hydrogen atoms for every one of oxygen. That arrangement is not changed when water is placed close to a magnet. But the arrangement of the molecules themselves in the water probably does change."

"Probably?" Angela asked. "Does it or doesn't it?"

"That change is debatable. I think it happens. I think the molecules all line up in certain ways, and that affects how the water reacts with other molecules. Other scientists say it doesn't, but in experiments it has been proven that plants that are watered with water that has sat in a magnetic container either die or don't do well."

"Then the water must change in some way," Angela said.

"That's what I say. The physicians your school board consulted with said I was talking pseudoscience. But there is one thing that is interesting

148

about Point Lake on the surface, that makes it different from any other lake in the area."

"What's that?"

"There are no fish in it. There never have been. No fish, no worms, no aquatic plants. Nothing."

"That's interesting," Angela said. "You think that would have sounded an alarm."

"It didn't. But let me continue. The magnetism was only one of the things that bothered me about the water in Point Lake. There is also a high concentration of an unidentified fossilized microorganism in and around the lake."

"Are you serious?" Angela asked.

"Yes."

"But I thought the water was thoroughly tested. I didn't read about an unidentified microorganism."

"And you won't read about it anywhere unless I write an article on the matter," Spark said matter-of-factly. "I've studied this particular organism more closely than anybody."

"But didn't other people know about the organism?" Angela asked. "I can't believe they'd let us drink water that had something deadly in it."

"Many people knew about the organism, although, except for me, nobody knows its specific qualities. Nobody considered it dangerous."

"Why not?" she asked.

"Because, as I said, it is a fossilized organism. It's dead. You cannot be infected by a dead organism."

"Then why were you concerned about the organism?" she asked.

Spark hesitated. "That question opens the door

149

to a mystery, or pseudo-science, depending on how you want to look at it." He paused. "I don't know if this is the time or place to go into it."

Angela leaned forward in her seat. "Please do. I won't put it in my article if you don't want me to."

"If it is of no use to your article, why do you want to hear about it?"

"Because I'm curious," Angela said honestly.

Spark considered. "What inspired you to write this article now, a year after the students' complaints?"

Angela stared him in the eye. "Students are getting sick again."

Spark raised an eyebrow. "I didn't know about that."

"We who go there know."

"Interesting," Spark said. "I read about that girl at Point High who shot her friends. Did that have anything to do with what we are discussing?"

"I think it did," Angela said.

"Could you elaborate?"

"First I'd like to hear what led you to believe that a dead organism could be unhealthy."

"Then you will tell me what is happening at the school?"

"I can tell you what I know," Angela said.

"Fair enough." Spark glanced at the door to make sure no one was listening in from the other room. "The organism concerned me because it was not in any book. It has a DNA structure unlike anything on record. In fact, I can go so far as to say it doesn't have DNA in the usual sense."

"Wait a second. If it is so different, wouldn't half the biologists in the country be studying it?"

Spark spoke with anger. "There are four full professors of biology here on this campus. I have been unable to persuade even one of them to peek at this organism."

"That seems absurd."

"You don't know how badly my reputation was tarnished by my protesting the use of Point Lake as a source of drinking water. When I approached my colleagues about the organism and told them how unique I thought it was, they weren't interested. They thought I was unstable at the least. But to be fair, it is not as if a biologist can glance in a microscope and note the unusual qualities of the organism. It has to be studied for some time. My colleagues didn't want to put in the time. But let me go on. Point Lake is not the only home of this particular organism."

"But you said it wasn't in any book."

"It isn't," he said. "But I have found it elsewhere."

"Where?" she asked.

"In Chile, in South America. High in the Andes."

Angela took in a sharp breath. "Where the other meteor crashed—the one that you mentioned in your article?"

"That is correct. It is currently called Lake Curro. But in the language of the Ropans who used to live there, it was known as Lake Sentia."

"Sethia," Angela whispered.

Spark sat up. "What did you say?"

"Nothing."

"I heard you. I see you have done your research. The Manton used to call Point Lake, Sethia, or Bath of Blood. The similarity in the names is disturbing, and I have no way of explaining it. Worse, I have no reasonable way of explaining why the histories of the two lakes are the same. The Manton considered Point Lake an evil place. They—"

"I have read the stories," Angela interrupted.

"I'm sure you have. You know about the KAtuu?"

"Yes. I do."

"You might be surprised to learn that the Ropans spoke of a similar race of beings that came from Lake Sentia. They were called the *Kalair.*"

"The names." Angela gasped.

"Again, similar. I know. It's peculiar, because the Manton and the Ropans have entirely different languages. But as far as the two meteor lakes were concerned, they were speaking the same language."

"What were the Kalair supposed to be like?" Angela asked.

"The legends depict them as being like the KAtuu in many respects. They were evil. They craved human flesh. They could transform people into creatures like themselves."

"Could they fly?"

"I know nothing about that attribute," Spark said.

"The Kalair were transformed human beings?" Angela asked.

Spark hesitated. "It is my understanding from

studying the Kalair myths that the original ones were not supposed to be from this planet."

"Which planet were they from?" Angela asked.

"Now we are way off the train of scientific conjecture."

"I don't care. Tell me what you know."

Spark shrugged. "The Ropans were excellent astronomers. They knew the planets orbited the sun before western civilization did. They believed the Kalair came from the fifth planet."

More humans would travel from the third planet to the fifth, and more of her kind would take birth.

Where did that come from? Her dream?

What an amazing coincidence.

As amazing as the coincidence of the names.

"Which planet is that?" Angela asked.

"The fifth planet from the sun right now is Jupiter. But the Kalair definitely could not have come from there. Jupiter is a gas giant. It has a poisonous atmosphere and a crushing gravitational field. Life as we know it could not evolve there. But . . ." Spark hesitated.

"What?"

"You have to understand that talk like this has little to do with scientific theory. It is more in the region of wild speculation."

"That doesn't bother me. This whole subject is wild."

"You have a point there," Spark said. "It is likely that in the past the fifth planet from the sun was not Jupiter, but another planet."

"Do they often switch places with each other?"

Spark chuckled. "No. But between Mars and Jupiter is the asteroid belt. It is commonly accepted that the asteroids are what is left of the original fifth planet."

"What happened to it?"

"No one knows. For one reason or another it blew up."

"When?" Angela asked.

"Most astronomers would say it was millions if not billions of years ago. They base that estimate on the time when many meteors hit the Earth. These ancient meteors, both large and small, are believed to have hit the Earth when the original fifth planet broke up."

"Do you believe that?" Angela asked.

"I believe that when the fifth planet exploded it threw good-size rocks our way. Most must have landed in the oceans. We see evidence of a few on land, however."

"Wait a second," Angela interrupted. "You said in your article that Point Lake was formed less than a hundred thousand years ago. You said that the lake in South America was formed at the same time."

"At about the same time, yes."

Angela saw what he was driving at, even though he was reluctant to say it aloud. "So you believe the fifth planet blew up then—not millions of years ago, but only a hundred thousand years ago. You think these two meteors came from that planet's breaking up."

Spark nodded in admiration. "You're perceptive.

Yes, I think the main meteoric bombardment of our planet was from another source, at a time near the formation of our solar system. But I think Point Lake and Lake Curro were formed by meteors that came from a planet that had life on it."

Angela almost jumped out of her chair. It was all coming together. "Because of the microorganisms?" she exclaimed.

Spark sighed. "Yes."

"Because it doesn't look as if they came from here!"

Spark sighed again. "Yes."

"Why does that depress you?"

"You have to understand the scientific view of life in the solar system. Besides Earth, Mars was the only planet thought to have a chance of having evolved life. But the findings of the *Voyager* probes made it appear unlikely that the place is anything but dead. My esteemed scientific colleagues would, therefore, be reluctant to sanction the theory that life had evolved on a world even farther from the sun than Mars, such as our original fifth planet."

"But it could have," Angela said.

"Yes, I think so. If the atmospheric conditions were ideal, the surface of the original fifth planet could have been every bit as warm as Earth is today."

"Then what's the problem? Why did they hound you out the door?"

"Because of what I mentioned a moment ago. That the fossilized microorganism has an extraterrestrial origin." Spark stopped and cleared his throat. "I made the mistake of suggesting the possibility in the wrong circle of people."

"But it seems a reasonable theory to me. Especially since the microorganism has only been found in the vicinity of these two meteor hits."

"I appreciate your support, believe me. But you have to understand the context in which these theories of mine were brought up against me. I was warning against using Point Lake as a source of drinking water for high school students. I had already published my article connecting Point Lake to Lake Curro. I had already spoken about the similar microorganisms located at the two places, although I had not written about them. The supporters of the school location—particularly the contractor who was to build the school—used that information to portray me as a charlatan. Little green bugs from outer space—they made it into a circus. They even tried to demolish the theory that a meteor had originally formed the lake, which of course was ridiculous." Spark paused to smile. "But that same contractor changed his mind when he tried to dig the foundation for the school. He could hardly cut into the ground, it was so hard. I heard he lost a lot of money on the job."

"I'd like to backtrack for a second," Angela said. "You said the experts were not concerned about the microorganism because it was dead. But you were concerned. Why?"

"I believe many organisms might have survived the impact of the meteor."

"Why?"

156

"Because I have researched the history of both lakes. Of course, I don't believe in the horror stories that have grown up around them. But I feel there must be something unsavory about the water in the lakes. The Mantons and the Ropans both got sick from drinking it. There has even been recent history concerning the dangers of Point Lake—from the early settlers in this area. To this day, in Chile, Lake Curro is completely shunned. It is seen as a source of illness. No one even lives near it. Also, there is the fact that there are no fish in *either* lake. But if you ask me if it is the organism or the magnetism that causes all these problems, I'd have to say I don't know for sure. If you ask me if the organism is from the fifth planet, I don't know. They are all intriguing theories. But I do know this for a fact: the kids who drank the most water from Point Lake were the ones who got sick."

"What do you mean, the most water?" Angela asked.

"It was hot last fall. The football team and the cheerleading squad practiced in that heat. They drank substantially more of that water than anybody else, and they were the kids who got sick."

"That's right." Angela had never put that together before, and it had been staring her right in the face. "So we have two possible sources of contaminants here—the magnetism and the organism."

"That's correct," Spark said.

"Is it possible they work together?"

"I don't understand your question."

"You said water that had been exposed to a

strong magnet was bad for plants and fish. Is it possible that the organism thrives in such water?"

"I never thought of that before, but I doubt it."

"Why?"

"Because living things don't appear to like such water."

"Living things on this planet," Angela said.

Spark was uncomfortable. "I would be extremely reluctant to put the two ideas together."

"Why? If the organism came here from a exploded planet, then it came here on a piece of home. Maybe the whole surface of the fifth planet was magnetic."

Spark was surprised at her wild postulating, although impressed. "You talk as if you've been there." He glanced at his watch. "I wish we could talk more, but a student of mine will be here in a few minutes. Before you go I'd like you to briefly describe what is happening at Point High."

Angela stood and thought for a minute. She had believed Mary was insane—even when she found the blood caked into the crack in the floor of the warehouse. Even when Jim had mingled his blood with hers and given her an appetite for red meat that couldn't be satisfied. It hadn't escaped her notice that there was more iron in red meat than in practically any other food. What was her body doing? Trying to change her into one huge polarized alien microorganism? It sure felt that way.

Angela now believed everything Mary had said was true.

"We've got a few monsters on the loose," Angela

told Professor Spark. "Their numbers grow daily. I might be turning into one myself. I sure hope not, but I've got cravings no teenage girl should have. I'm so hungry right now I could eat you alive. I know you'll think that's crazy, but remember how people thought you were crazy to connect the two lakes? Don't toss out those stories about the KAtuu and the Kalair too quickly. There's a lot of truth in them."

Spark was stunned. "Are you saying you're sick, too?"

Angela threw her head back and laughed. "I had a dream last night that I was an astronaut who came back to Earth after a visit to the fifth planet and ate my best friends. Then I changed into a huge batlike monster and was eventually hunted down by men with laser guns. Sounds pretty corny, huh? Except my new boyfriend's a member of Point High's football team. He's the quarterback. He drank a lot of that bad water. I think he might be quarterbacking the whole show. His name's Jim Kline, and he's the guy Mary Blanc was trying to kill when the police stopped her. I helped them, for God's sake. I saved Jim's life. But you know what?" She leaned closer. "I wish now I had let her kill the bastard."

"Angela—" Spark began.

"Thank you for your time, professor," Angela said, turning away. "I've got to go. I've got to eat."

She ran from the room, and it was well for him that he didn't try to stop her. All of a sudden he had begun to smell too good to resist.

159

ANGELA HEARD ON THE RADIO—OF ALL PLACES—THAT Mary Blanc had been released on half a million dollars bail. *On a Sunday for godsake,* Angela thought. Nguyen had been right about how good her lawyer was. Angela was sitting in a McDonald's eating three extremely rare Big Macs—and finding them far from satisfactory—when she got the news. A couple of fourteen-year-old boys sat across from her with a ghetto blaster. She grabbed it out of their hands when she heard Mary's name. But the newscaster made no mention of where Mary was going, except to say that she had to remain in the area.

"Hey," one of the boys protested. "That's ours."

She smiled. They were both rather plump, which she thought made them more attractive somehow. It might be fun to—squeeze them. She handed them back their boom box and gave the one who had spoken a pat on the head.

"Eat your food and keep your mouth shut, little boy," she said sweetly.

Angela got back in her car and drove to the expressway. She had an idea where Mary would be hiding out. Her family owned a cabin in a forested area outside of Kemp, which lay roughly between the University of Michigan and Point. Angela had been there twice. It wouldn't be too far out of her way to swing by the cabin and have a long talk with Mary about the KAtuu and the missing fifth planet and the long kiss Jim had given her in the middle of the lake. They could join forces. They could be a team. They could save the world.

But Mary might kill me when it's all over.

Angela would not put it past her.

She found the door to Mary's cabin lying wide open when she came to a halt at the end of the long gravel driveway. The cabin was nestled in the midst of a thick forest. The nearest neighbor was half a mile away. Flies buzzed around Angela's head as she got out of her car.

"Hello?" she called. "Mary?"

Oh, God.

There was a foot inside a black shoe lying in the cabin doorway. It was a man's leg, and it was attached to a man's body. Angela took a step closer, then stopped and grimaced. Already, with only half the body in view, she could see a dark puddle of blood had formed around the guy. Yeah, he was real dead, like the two at the party last week. Another step closer and she could see that he had a hole in his chest that only a close-range shotgun blast could have caused. He lay on his back with his mouth and eyes open and flies crawling all over him. Angela recognized the man—Officer Martin, one of the cops who had helped Nguyen capture Mary. Mary obviously had not appreciated his efforts.

But the obvious was not always right. She had assumed Mary had done the guy so she could escape and go after the monsters. But another step into the cabin showed Angela a sight that outdid all the horrors she had witnessed in the last few days.

Mary, dressed in blue jeans and a bloodstained T-shirt, was hanging by the neck from a thin wire. She had on brown leather boots; the right one was beginning to slip off her foot. The blood was from the gaping wound the wire had cut into her neck. Darn, tied that thing too tight while I was trying to commit suicide. That's what the evidence was supposed to tell everybody. Killed the cop, then felt guilty and decided to buy the big one by going for a swing after jumping off the nearby couch. Why, the shotgun was lying right there on the floor beneath Mary. Angela bet it even had Mary's fingerprints on the trigger.

Angela moaned. "No, Mary." She closed her eyes and cried. "No."

Angela didn't believe the evidence. In the last few days she had learned a thing or two about those who had drunk too deeply from the lake. They had unique appetites. Angela reopened her eyes. The puddle around the cop was not big considering the extent of his wound. The stain on Mary's shirt was not that wide given the incision in her neck. The

KAtuu couldn't resist having a little snack—drinking a little blood—in the midst of business.

Angela wished she hadn't thought about food right then. The next tragedy started with good intentions. She decided she couldn't just leave her friend hanging there. She fetched a chair from the kitchen and placed it below Mary's feet. She didn't believe she'd have the strength to lift enough of Mary's weight off the wire in order to pull the noose off of her friend's head. But either Mary had lost more weight in prison than either of them had realized or else Angela Warner was now one strong babe. Angela had the wire off in seconds. She cradled Mary in her arms as they slumped to the carpeted floor. Beautiful Mary—Angela had always been so jealous of her shiny brown hair, her huge green eyes. At least Mary had had a chance to close them before the end had come. Angela buried her face in Mary's face and washed her friend's blood with her tears.

You were the brave one. You went after them alone. You didn't ask for help, and when you were stopped you didn't complain. You were great. I will always remember you as great, even if the world will always despise you. I'm not you, I can't be you, but I swear I will not rest until what you began is finished. Until every one of those blood-sucking bastards is lying in the dirt with a hole in his heart.

"Mary," Angela cried, uncontrollable sobs shaking her body. But these tremors had another cause besides grief. Angela couldn't stop shaking because she was hungry. She was holding her dead friend, her dead best friend, and she couldn't stop thinking about how good it would be to lean over and open her mouth and . . .

"I won't do it!" she screamed.

Still she couldn't let go of Mary. She couldn't get up and run from the cabin and save what was left of her sanity. She closed her eyes and felt the edge of the incision in Mary's neck with her fingertips. Then she took the bloody fingers and pressed them to her own lips. And the thrill that went through her body was sexual in intensity. An incomparably ancient longing quenched for an instant in time. She sighed with pleasure and touched Mary's wound again—lightly and with respect—and lifted the fingers once more to her lips. The elixir Jim had let her taste. She sucked on her fingers hungrily. Harder and harder. Wanting to get the last drop.

So hard she began to eat her own hand.

"Angela," a voice said,

She opened her eyes with a start. Lieutenant Nguyen stepped into the room. Funny, she hadn't heard him drive up. Quickly she wiped the blood off her mouth.

Don't mind me, I was just drinking my friend's blood.

"Hello," she said.

Nguyen surveyed the scene and was forced to close his eyes. When he reopened them he was the color of chalk. He stepped to her side and peered down at her.

"What happened here?" he asked.

"Jim Kline was here," she said.

"You saw him?"

"No."

"How do you know, then?"

"It's a long story." She eased Mary off her lap and onto the floor. She would have liked to kiss her friend goodbye, but not with company in the room. Nguyen helped her to her feet. "Have you been following me?" Angela asked.

"Yes. Did you know?"

"No."

"Tell me what happened," Nguyen repeated.

Angela stared him in the eye, and suddenly she felt a power go up her spine and into her head and out from her as if she were a magnetic field with claws. The strange thing was that it didn't surprise her when it happened. It was as if it were a psychic muscle that had always been there, even before the madness had started, and she had simply never used it before. The power gave her new sensitivity; she felt as if she held Nguyen's mind in her palm. She couldn't read his thoughts, but she could *touch* them as if they were made of matter. She suspected she could make him believe what she wanted him to believe just by holding his eye and talking in a certain way.

"I can't," she said simply.

Nguyen blinked. "What's happened to you, Angela?"

She swiped at her mouth again. She had missed a bit of the blood. "I've become a naughty little girl. I think I lost my virginity last night. I lost something, that's for sure." Her eyes bored into him—inside his brain she could actually *feel* his confusion, his horror of her—and he took an involuntary step back. "Let me go, Nguyen," she said softly. "Quit following me. Let me do what I have to do. By the time you know enough to believe what is happening you'll be dead."

He was sweating heavily. He gasped, "I don't know what you're talking about."

Staring down at Mary one last time, she said, "For your sake I hope you never do."

Angela left the cabin. Nguyen didn't try to stop her.

When she got home Plastic was waiting for her at the front door. She ran inside without pausing to shut the door behind her and went into the bathroom, where she saw in the mirror someone she hardly recognized. Wild blue eyes, the color of Earth's sky. But what color would the sky be that she would look out from tomorrow? She still had Mary's blood all over her, on her nose, in her hair.

"Christ," she swore. She turned on the water, scalding hot, and splashed it on her face again and again, all the while crying pitifully. Her fingers were bleeding from where she had bitten them; nevertheless, she pounded the countertop with her fists and heard it crack. She didn't want to be like them! She would kill them! She would kill herself first!

"Oh, go away," Angela moaned. Plastic had come into the bathroom and was trying to lick her hand. She had never seen the dog so friendly. Plastic must have known she was upset. Angela knelt to pet the dog on the head and scratch the fur on her back—Plastic just loved to be scratched. But the heat of the dog's tongue, the faint scent wafting off it. Why, it smelled of beef blood. Plastic must have been chewing on her bone just before Angela drove up. Oh, why, Angela asked herself as her brain once more began to do the unthinkable voodoo dance of death, couldn't the dog have been eating dry dog food? Just the smell of the blood—Angela didn't want to.

"I'm sorry," Angela cried.

She grabbed the dog hard. It began to fidget, then to whimper. Angela reached around and dug her nails into the dog's neck. Plastic started to cry, heart-piercing wails that Angela tried to quiet by reaching deep inside the dog's mouth. She was going to snap Plastic's face into two pieces. . . .

"Angie," a voice said.

Angela let go of the dog, and Plastic dashed away as if she had a devil on her tail. Angela was breathing heavily. She looked up, although it was not necessary; she had recognized the voice.

"Hello, Jim," she said.

He knelt in front of her, looking so good. A healthy young man with his whole life in front of him. Maybe he'd live to be a hundred thousand years old; she didn't know. He'd probably have huge, leathery wings by then, and purple talons. His fingernails were black as ink already. He was holding the note her grandfather had left her the previous morning. Now she wondered why it had been typed as Jim handed it to her.

"I wrote this," he said.

She glanced at her grandfather's closed door. He never shut it when he went out. He always laughed and said that at his age he had nothing to hide. Jim had probably eaten him immediately after their first date. Sneaked back into the house and didn't even bother to stop and give his sleeping beauty a kiss. But maybe he had done her that small favor before he had stolen away another huge chunk of her existence. Maybe it was a kiss that had bestowed upon her the vision of the alien world. No, it was his blood. His blood was a concentrated form of the contaminated water.

"I understand," she whispered. Her lower lip trembled, and she bit it and sucked on the blood. Jim put his hand on her shoulder. There was no warmth. A huge crab claw would have been more comforting.

"Mary's dead," he said.

"Yes."

"You're one of us now," he said.

"I understand."

"There are lots of us."

She looked up. "I'd like to meet them."

"Whenever you want."

"Tonight would be good." She forced a smile. "I'd like to have a party here for all of us."

CHAPTER XI

ANGELA SAT ALONE IN THE HOUSE ON HER GRAND-father's bed. It was three in the afternoon. Jim had left a few minutes before. The party was set for eight. She couldn't have it any earlier because she had things to do to prepare for her visitors, and she was going to do them. Jim hadn't cleaned up after killing her grandfather. What remained of her father's dad was not pleasant to view. It was amazing that she hadn't noticed the smell, but then Jim had stuffed sheets under the door to prevent the stench from circulating to the rest of the house. She shuddered to think what would have happened if Kevin had peeked into her grandfather's room while he had been in the house the previous morn-ing. Sweet Kevin—she wondered if she would ever see him again.

A tear ran down her cheek, followed by a sniffle and another tear. She hadn't known her grandfa-ther well, but what she had known she had loved. He had been the only one who'd wanted to take her in when things were tough at home. He'd been happy to have her stay with him. She remembered the day he picked her up at the airport with his latest girlfriend on his arm. She had thought the woman was a second cousin to her or something. She had loved his love, so full of life, so free, so nonjudgmental.

But what did *they* know about love? It didn't satisfy their hunger; therefore, it was useless to them. Their existence seemed incredibly one-dimensional to her. Since that was the case, she doubted they were very smart. She had sure fooled Jim easily enough. He thought she was one of them just because she had tried to eat her dog. So her tastes had changed a little. Jim's walking in at that exact moment had been fortunate. He had seen her at her worst and now he trusted her. Now she would have them *all* in one place. Mary had never had such an opportunity. Angela suspected Mary had greatly underestimated their numbers.

Angela had already decided she was going to blow up the house when she got them all inside. Since she didn't have dynamite, she'd have to do it with gasoline. She couldn't count on being able to detonate the propane tank. Jim had run into it with his truck, and nothing had happened. Sure, if she rigged it with a five-gallon bottle of gas, it would probably blow. But the tank was outside the house, where everyone parked. Because there would be a bright moon, they'd see it if she used such an obvious device. The only place to plant a bomb was in the basement. It was normally closed off from the rest of the house; no one would go down there during the party.

She didn't know the exact firepower she'd get per gallon of gasoline, but she figured that if she could obtain twelve five-gallon water bottles and fill them to the brim with gas, she'd be able to kill everybody in the house. If the propane tank blew at the same time, so much the better.

But she didn't want to die with the others. Jim had already contaminated her with his blood. It must have been his blood that was changing her, because she'd never gone through the heavy water-drinking stage that the others had. Still she would probably end up like the rest of them. But she had to give herself a chance. Maybe she could learn to resist the urge to kill even if her body insisted that she feed. She couldn't just light the bomb and have it go off in her face.

She needed a fuse. A two-minute delay at least.

Unfortunately, she didn't have a box of unused fireworks lying around. She'd have to make her own. But with what? She couldn't take a long piece of rope and soak it in gasoline. The flame would jump too quickly along the rope and kill her before she could get back up the steps. Plus the gasoline would smell. She guessed that improved physical strength wouldn't be the only benefit of the human-to-monster transformation. Their senses, including smell, would probably be heightened far beyond the normal human range. She'd have to be careful to wipe all gasoline off the bottles before she sealed them and brought them into the house.

Gunpowder was what she'd need to make a fuse. It, too, would give off a powerful odor, but only once it started burning. Bullet shells had gunpowder in them; shotgun shells had more. If she could get enough of the latter and get the shot out of them, she could lay down a long enough line on the basement floor to give her time to get out of the house. She could place a piece of rope leading right up to the center bottle of gasoline, which would have a paper cap on top of it with more gunpowder. The stuff would burn through the cap in a second. Then *bang*—no more Mr. and Mrs. Monster.

Angela flashed a faint smile at the bloody mess in the bedroom.

It was good to have a plan.

It would be even better to watch them die.

Angela collected her purse and left the house. She didn't have to clean up her grandfather's bedroom —at this party the mess might even be a drawing card. She worried briefly what she should serve them, then laughed at the absurdity of the idea. What should she plan to serve a bunch of cannibals who were only interested in one thing? Well, she wasn't inviting any of her other friends over to meet these new kids in town.

Before she was able to do anything she had to stop to eat. She bought four pounds of steak and ate half of it in the car in the market parking lot. The pounding in her head diminished; it didn't go away, though. That worried her. Even if she survived the blast—how could she live like this?

"I'll have to face that when the time comes," she whispered to herself as she wiped her hands off on the bag that held the other two steaks. She had also bought a bottle of Tylenol; she popped four pills before starting the car and swallowed them dry. She doubted they'd help. They didn't.

It was ironic where she was heading to steal the empty five-gallon water bottles—Point High. The faculty apparently drank bottled water. *Maybe that's why they eat so little red meat,* she thought. Anyway, she'd seen the bottles in the back near the guys' showers. There was a whole pile of them, if she remembered correctly. The water guy must have a huge route and only stopped by occasionally, she thought.

Fifteen minutes later Angela discovered that her "whole pile" equaled only eight empty bottles. That was forty gallons of gasoline. A lot, but would it be enough? Who the hell knew? She was stuck on the idea of having at least sixty gallons. It was already close to four—no time to fool around. She had to get to the sporting good store in the mall in Balton by five to get the shotgun shells. She'd worry about her other containers on the way home.

She made it to the mall by twenty after four. The shells were stacked behind the counter. She had picked a bad week to buy them. After all, a girl her age had killed two people with a shotgun only the week before. The guy at the counter looked as if he had just gotten out of the army. He had a blond crew cut, square shoulders, a rod up his spine—the whole bit. He wanted to know what she wanted the twenty boxes of shells for.

"They're for my grandfather," she said.

"Is he with you?" the guy asked.

"No."

"What does he shoot?"

"He target-practices, mainly. Is there a problem? I'm eighteen. I have ID."

"I'd like to see it," the guy said. Angela showed him her license. He studied it closely—he seemed to be memorizing her name. "You're from Chicago?" he asked.

"I moved her last June," she said.

The guy blinked. Something had struck him. "Hey, is your grandfather Mike Warner?"

She smiled, although it was forced beyond belief. "Yeah. Do you know him?"

The guy slapped his knee. "Hell, he used to go out with my sister."

Angela winced. "Your sister? How old is your sister?" The guy himself couldn't have been thirty.

"She's younger than me." He chuckled. "He was a great guy, though. She really liked him. How's he doing?"

She swallowed. "Oh, he's still up to his old tricks."

"He bought himself a shotgun? I don't think he had one when he was dating Dorothy."

"He hasn't had it long."

The guy began to stack up the boxes of shells on the counter. He wasn't worried about her anymore. Twenty boxes. "Tell him hello for me. The name's Sam. Tell him Dorothy still says he was the best."

Angela had to lower her head. "I will."

Before Sam finished ringing up her order she added a hundred feet of rope, a tube of glue, and a razor-sharp hunting knife. She had nothing at home to cut open the shells; all the stuff in the kitchen was dull. Besides, she thought, the knife might come in handy.

She drove around Balton for half an hour but couldn't find any more five-gallon water bottles. At a supermarket she bought eight two-and-a-half-gallon containers—they were much more common —and also picked up a plastic funnel. She had decided how she would get enough gasoline.

There were three stations in Point. She had a fifteen-gallon tank in her Camry. She could fill up the tank, drive the car home, and angle it up on some rocks to drain the gasoline directly into the bottles with the help of the funnel, leaving herself just enough fuel to get back to a station. Sixty gallons—four tankfuls. Then she'd be set.

The thought of revenge drove her on, but she felt terrible anxiety about the evening. The stakes were high—how high she didn't like to guess. The death of the community? The end of the human race? Jesus. There were a dozen things that could go wrong. As she drove back toward Point she resolved that if she had to—if it looked as if even one of them would escape—she would forget the fuse, put her lighter directly to the gasoline, and be the first to go. Kevin would just have to forgive her. She knew how much he'd miss her. She thought about him a lot as she worked, and about Mary, too. Great people—she'd been lucky to meet them. She wished she could go to Kevin for help now, but she vowed to herself that he wouldn't be brought into it. He'd never believe her and would just end up being killed.

Angela filled up at the station closest to her house. At her grandfather's place she easily steered the left side of her car up onto the rocks. The stones worked as well as jacks and left the bottom of the gas tank exposed. She was able to slide one of her empty five-gallon bottles directly under the bottom cap on the tank. Then she ran into a problem—or rather, she realized she was going to have a problem before it materialized. Once she took off the cap, how was she supposed to stop the flow of gasoline while she positioned the next bottle? She debated the issue for several minutes without coming up with a brilliant solution. She was still extremely worried about spilling gasoline close to the house.

What she eventually did was *slowly* unscrew the cap. Near the end of the cap strip the gas began to trickle out. She undid it just a tiny bit more. Better to be patient at this stage, she cautioned herself. The gasoline dribbled into her funnel and began to fill the bottle. It took her five minutes to empty five gallons. She retightened the cap while she reached for the next bottle, spilling only a few drops. They'd have to have noses like wolves to get a whiff of the stuff, she thought.

It was funny, but it was only then that she paused to ask herself what *they* would be called if they were to be named by someone in the twentieth century. They craved human flesh but prefered to eat people alive—that made them ghouls or zombies. In a sense they were from outer space—that made them aliens. But they liked human blood—*she* liked human blood, for god's sake—and if the myths and her nightmares were true, they mutated into batlike beings.

"Yeah," she said to herself as she resumed her task, "they're vampires. It's too bad they were here before there were crucifixes or garlic, or I could forget all about this bomb business and just get myself to the religious store and the supermarket."

Angela filled close to three bottles—she left herself just enough gas to get around to the other side of the lake—and went searching for the next station. She kept an eye on her rearview mirror the whole time, on the lookout for Nguyen. She doubted he was still tailing her. What he had seen at Mary's cabin had scared him—it would have scared any normal person into a mental hospital. And that thing she had done to him just before she left felt as if she had locked his brain neurons in a pattern she chose. It came to her then that Jim had been using the same power on her from the start of his seduction. She liked to think she hadn't come that close to screwing him on the first date without *some* kind of supernatural influence. The goddam bloodsucker. How come they didn't sell birth control to protect girls like her from guys like him?

Gee, they might sell them soon. They might be the next big market in birth control. Keep those micro-organisms from growing in you, girls! Save money on your groceries at the same time! Practice safe necking! Wear Count Condoms! The only ones he can't bite through!

"I am sick," she muttered.

It was also sick how he still had a sexual hold on her after all he had done to ruin her life and the lives of those she loved. Even while she was in the middle of plotting his destruction her thoughts turned to his kisses, his touch, his body. God, she couldn't let her imagination run down that yellow brick road, or it would constantly be stopping behind the bushes for a quickie. What was craziest of all was that she didn't know if she was still a virgin. Had they done it in the middle of the lake last night? While she was having her nightmare? Was she going to have a two-fanged baby in nine months that needed ten blood transfusions a day just to keep its color?

Angela took care of her eight five-gallon bottles, then dumped the water from her two-and-a-halfers into the lake and started on them. They were harder to fill because the openings were smaller. But unlike the five-gallon bottles, they had caps, which she replaced after they were filled. The bigger bottles she capped with tin foil.

Except for one—one that she had left only half full. She knew a thing or two about how gasoline exploded. It was the *fumes* that caused ignition. Stick a match directly into a gallon of gasoline and most likely the match would go out. Her half-empty bottle would be her detonator. She would tie the other bottles tightly around it with her rope and

178

lead her trail of gunpowder to the top of it. *Bang, bang*—they would all go off in the same second.

She got one question at the last gas station she went to, which had also been the first station she had visited eighty minutes before. The guy wanted to know what she had done with her first tankful. Angela just smiled.

"I need a tune-up bad," she said. "Getting terrible mileage."

She had no trouble carrying the bottles inside and stacking them in the corner of the basement. She *was* stronger. But the smaller bottles—they didn't quite fit with the big ones. She put them aside for a moment while she set to work on the shotgun shells. She would figure out what to do with them later.

That was the fun part—getting the fuse ready. The gunpowder reminded her of past Fourths of July—happier times. It helped her to think about the past. She couldn't think about the future, and the present was too oppressive. Tears streaked her face—yeah, she was having a grand time. She'd seen too much blood but hadn't drunk enough! She was literally dying for a drink of the red stuff. Just a sip, but she wouldn't kill to get it. She had taken a vow about that, she reminded herself.

Her head throbbed as her heart broke and her throat cracked on bitter grief. She tried singing to keep up her spirits. *"They did the monster mash. It was a graveyard smash."* *"It's my party, and I'll cry if I want to."*

But it was all a bad joke, and she wasn't laughing.

The hell with them. I'm not serving appetizers. I'll bury what's left of Grandfather in the trees. I'll wash his sheets. They'll enter a clean house. They won't leave it though.

"They won't leave," she muttered as she finished with the fuse and once more picked up one of the smaller bottles, wondering where to put it.

CHAPTER XII

LIEUTENANT NGUYEN STOOD IN THE EMPTY WAREHOUSE and stared at the dust-free circle on the concrete floor. He wasn't alone. Officer Williams stood nearby holding a flashlight focused on the floor. Williams was not like Martin. He preferred to be called by his first name—Kenny—and he was new to the force, not a wily old devil like Martin. Of course, few cops ever got as tough as Martin had been, even after twenty years on the force. Yet Martin hadn't been tough enough to stop what was happening from killing him. Nguyen wondered if *he* was. He kind of doubted it.

Nguyen didn't know why he'd come to the warehouse again. He had already visited it the day before—Saturday—after Angela and her friend had made him aware of its importance. He had found the dried blood in the crack in the floor, as they had undoubtedly likewise discovered. But unlike them, he had been able to have the blood analyzed. It had come from four separate people, as Mary had said. Only an hour earlier he had received a computer report that matched the blood to the blood types of four missing people—two men and two women who had been on their way to the West Coast and who had only stopped in Balton for a drink. Nguyen tried to remember if Mary had suspected Jim and his pals of stalking only those who were from out of town. She had made so many other surprisingly accurate remarks—in retrospect.

Then again, Mary had said they were dealing with monsters.

"If you were to stand here and scream, Kenny," Nguyen said, "do you think someone listening outside could hear you?"

Kenny shifted uncomfortably. He had already commented on the bad vibes of the place. Nguyen didn't know much about vibes, but he sure knew when he didn't like someone, and he had hated Jim Kline from the start. If that kid had killed Martin, he was going to pay for it, and in a bad way. Nguyen would see to it, and he would make it look legal. There were always ways.

"I doubt it," Officer Kenny Williams said, glancing around in the dark. "This is a big place. You'd have to scream awfully loud."

Nguyen knelt and touched the dried blood. As soon as he did he knew why he'd returned to the warehouse. He needed to see once again that what he was dealing with was real, since he hadn't fully returned to his senses after his encounter with Angela at Mary's cabin. First there had been Martin lying on the floor with his guts hanging out.

Poor Mike—Nguyen knew his first name. It had stung to see the flies crawling on his friend's face. Suddenly the war seemed like only yesterday; he thought he had left it all behind.

This is worse than anything that happened in Nam. There the enemy had a name. You could see them coming. They were like everyone else.

Then he had seen Mary lying dead in Angela's arms, the apparent victim of a suicide. That had added another layer of unreality to the situation. But Nguyen could have dealt with all of this, even though it caused him pain. But not Angela. Angela not just holding her dead friend, but touching her, wiping the blood off her incision and putting it into her mouth. That was too much.

"Dear God," Nguyen whispered. He felt sick, scared. He had never been this scared, even in the heat of battle with bullets whizzing over his head. Angela had let go of Mary and stood and met his gaze straight, and Nguyen had felt as if he were being hypnotized by a vulture. It was unthinkable that he had let her walk away. But then, in that place, there hadn't been a chance in hell he could have stopped her.

"Quit following me. Let me do what I have to do. By the time you know enough to believe what's happening, you'll already be dead."

He still didn't know enough, and now, finally, he had to ask himself if he wanted to know. But he'd been the one who'd had to tell Martin's wife her husband was dead. He had done the same thing many times in Nam, and then it had steeled him to go on. To get the job done, to drive off the enemy. Of course, the enemy had kept coming and had finally driven him away.

But not this time.

He wiped the dried blood off on his pants leg and stood up. He turned to Williams. "The identity of the four victims has been established beyond doubt?" he asked.

"That's what the FBI says," Williams replied.

"How old were they?"

"I believe they ranged in age from twenty-two to twenty-six."

"Is the bureau coming in on this?" Nguyen asked.

"Not yet." Williams added, "They want to see what else you come up with."

"Who's this mortician you told me about earlier?"

Williams pulled a pad of paper from his back pocket. He studied it in the beam of the flashlight. "His name is Kane. He wants to speak to you about the bodies of the boy and the girl Mary Blanc killed last week."

"They were buried a few days ago," Nguyen said.

"I know, and he knows that. But he still wants to speak to you. He says it's urgent. I asked him why, but he insisted on speaking only to you. He said you could get him at work tonight. He's there late."

"I hope he won't be working too late in the next few days," Nguyen said grimly. He turned toward the warehouse door. "Let's get out of here, Kenny."

* * *

They began to arrive promptly at eight. They came individually. Angela met each one at the door. At first she welcomed them and asked if they wanted anything to eat, but since they didn't smile in response or appear hungry, she quit. When there was a knock at the door she just went over and opened it and let them in. No one spoke; it was like no party she'd ever been to. Everyone just sat and stared at one another. Many sat on the floor. To say that they gave her the creeps was not saying it strongly enough. Their eyes were dark. They reminded her of bats that had hung too long in a cold cave. Even when they sat and looked around they didn't seem to see much with their physical eyes. Yet they seemed to radiate something akin to radar. Subtle vibrations swept back and forth across the room that she couldn't quite catch. She didn't know what they were picking up from her.

Mary had been way off in her estimates. Angela had half the football team and every one of the cheerleaders at her house. There was no one outside those two groups, though. Talk about cliques and peer pressure. You must eat your neighbor, Angie. Everyone's doing it.

Angela sat near the door with her head down and played butler. She had two Bic lighters in her pockets and sweaty palms. Where the hell was Jim? Why was he, of all monsters, late?

She was so terribly hungry. The pounding in her brain—would it never stop?

Finally Jim arrived, and when he did Angela's heart stopped in her chest. Jim had not come alone.

Kevin was with him—Kevin, with his big innocent smile. Jim must have talked to him in his human voice the whole way to her house. Jim came in behind Kevin and closed the door.

"A and W," Kevin said. "How come you didn't tell me about your party?"

Angela had to fight to regain her voice. "Why is he here?" she asked Jim.

"Why not?" Jim asked, his expression flat.

"Angie," Kevin said, hurt.

"He's not one of us," Angela said sharply to Jim. "Get him out of here."

"No," Jim said.

"Why not?" Angela demanded.

"Excuse me," Kevin said. "How come I'm not one of you?"

"We need him," Jim said.

"What for?" Angela asked, although she had a sick feeling she knew the answer to that question. Jim's answer only made her more sick.

"For you," Jim said.

Angela grabbed Kevin's arm and pulled him toward the door. "Get out of here. We're not having a party, and you're not invited. I'm sick of you always bugging me. Go annoy some other girl."

"Stop," Jim said.

"Yeah, stop," Kevin said, shaking free. But he began to get suspicious—Angela could see it in his face—when Jim moved between them, separating her from Kevin. Angela had experienced the growth of her supernormal strength all day, but she knew she was no match for Jim. He was menacing, and Kevin cowered before him, although he tried to put up a brave front. He poked Jim playfully in the chest. "What's wrong?" he asked. "Haven't had anybody to eat today?"

"Not yet," Jim said. He raised his right hand and struck Kevin, hard, on the side of the head. Kevin didn't have a chance to react. He slammed into the wall and crumpled onto the floor, unconscious. Jim turned to Angela, who was frozen in horror.

"Have you had anything to eat today?" Jim asked.

Angela ran. She didn't know where she was going and as a result didn't get far. One of the others tripped her, and she sprawled onto the floor. Back on her knees, ready to make another dash for it, she was struck by something hard and powerful on the side of the head. Like Kevin she was slammed into the wall, and she crumpled to the floor. She didn't immediately lose consciousness, though. Rolling onto her back, she saw them gathered around her, ten-foot-tall statues from the wax museum of horrors. Sticky warm fluid slid over the side of her face. Jim knelt and touched her head. When he withdrew his fingers they were red. He touched them to his lips, tasting her.

"Almost ready," he said.

Angela blacked out.

Mortician Kane met Lieutenant Nguyen at the back door of his establishment. Kane resembled a corpse more than a live man, Nguyen thought. The man was elderly, white haired, with an unnaturally smooth red face—he had on a thick layer of makeup—and smelled heavily of cologne. Better than embalming fluid, Nguyen figured. He had big, moist, pale blue eyes; they appeared to be made of glass. Nguyen didn't understand how someone could grow up wanting to be a mortician. But he supposed it was good someone had such an inclination.

"I'm so happy you could come," Kane said, using both palms to shake Nguyen's hand. Nguyen had called him a few minutes earlier and told him he was on his way. He was alone because he had told Kenny Williams to go home to his wife and kids. If he could help it, he wasn't going to lose any more men this weekend.

"No problem," Nguyen said, stepping into the man's laboratory. Twin stainless steel tables glistened beneath harsh white lights. The body of an old lady lay on the far one. She was dressed in a long white wedding dress and had on ruby-colored slippers. Kane had obviously been doing her makeup when he stopped to answer the door. Kane led him past the woman.

"That's Mrs. Bevin," Kane said. "She made a vow to her husband to reenact their wedding once they were in heaven."

"Her husband approved of this?" Nguyen asked, gesturing to the white gown.

"I don't know. He's dead. He died many years ago."

"I see," Nguyen said. "What did you want to show me?"

"These," Kane said, stopping in front of twin metal containers set on a waist-level table. They were cylinder-shaped, both about four feet tall and a foot in diameter. Even before Kane removed the lid of the one on the right, Nguyen got a whiff of the repulsive odor. It was unlike anything he had smelled before, and yet it reminded him of a smell he'd experienced many times in Nam. The stench of death, of decay, of life lost. Yet this was worse than any rotting body on the battlefield.

"My Lord," Nguyen said, taking a step back.

"I should have warned you," Kane apologized. "I use these containers to hold the blood I drain from bodies before I embalm them. I used this particular container for the blood of both of the teenagers who were killed at the party. I understand that you are in charge of that case?"

"That is correct."

"Has the girl said why she did it?" Kane asked.

"The matter is still under investigation."

"I understand," Kane said quickly. "Anyway, I drained the blood of both these young people and put it in this container. That was on Monday, the day before the funerals. Ordinarily I dispose of the blood immediately—the same day. But I was unexpectedly called out of town on a business appointment and was late taking care of the matter. In fact, it was only today, while working on Mrs. Bevin, that I remembered I had yet to get rid of the material." He frowned and nodded to the container he had uncovered a moment ago. "But when I went to pour it away it was gone."

"The blood?" Nguyen asked.

"Yes."

"Perhaps you disposed of it and forgot."

"Impossible," Kane said. He cleared his throat. "I believe the blood was stolen. The lock on my back door had been forced open when I returned from my business trip on Thursday."

"I hadn't noticed."

"I had the lock fixed immediately. I cannot have my establishment unlocked at any time. If I were to have one body stolen, it would permanently ruin my reputation."

"I can imagine," Nguyen said. "Were there any bodies here while you were gone?"

"No."

"Who do you think took the blood?"

Kane was disappointed. "I was hoping you might be able to shed some light on the matter."

"I'm sorry, I can't." Nguyen gestured to the empty container. He assumed it was empty; he couldn't see over the top of it. "What's making that awful smell?"

"That's the other reason I called you out. There was something in the blood of those kids who were killed."

"What do you mean?"

"I'll show you." Kane took a pair of gloves from his back pocket and put them on. He reached up and tilted the container slightly, being careful not to let it topple. A mass of what could have been dark green algae was growing inside—the stench unbelievable. Nguyen felt his eyes burning and took another step back.

"What is that?" he asked, repulsed.

"I don't know," Kane said gravely. "In forty years of experience I have never seen anything like it. I tell you those teenagers' blood was contaminated."

"With what?" Nguyen demanded.

"I don't know."

"Some kind of organism must have grown in the container on the blood that remained."

Kane was firm. "No. I realize my leaving the blood in the container for so long before disposing of it must give you the impression that I am careless. But I assure you that I am seldom anything but a perfectionist. I sterilized these two containers before I embalmed the two teenagers. There were no organisms in the containers at that time. I could swear to that in court. Also, whatever is growing in here is very unusual." Kane tilted the can more on its side, revealing a portion of the backside. A narrow trail of the green stuff had made its way down the rear of the container. The trail led across the short distance to the second container. Nguyen had to lean over to see where it was heading and was surprised to find it had already crawled halfway up the back of the second container, which appeared to be well sealed.

Crawled? It's not an animal.

Nguyen didn't like to think it was an animal.

"What's in this other container?" Nguyen asked.

"Mrs. Bevin's blood."

"Interesting."

"Yes, indeed." Kane was grim. "It's as if this green matter is hunting her blood." He leaned closer. "Whoever stole the blood from this container wanted it for some special purpose."

CHAPTER XIII

ANGELA DREAMED OF THE ALIEN WORLD. THE DAY THE
World died. The World remembered it well. Yes,
even its own end. Because the World was unique. It
could die and be reborn. The mind of the World
took birth in Angela's mind in the nightmare. She
saw what it saw. She felt its shock, its terror, as the
men from the third planet, the one they called
Earth, appeared to erect their mighty machine.

The World was almost helpless against this inva-
sion. The men from the third planet had been
warned and didn't at first allow their silver space
ships to land on the surface. They knew what the
surface of the World could do, how the infection
could get inside them and begin to eat them unless
they ate others of their own kind. That's what
brought on the victim's hunger. The parasite had to
be fed, or else it would feed on its host. It hungered
for the living iron in the dying blood—to bring
about the polarity, the magnetism, that led to union
with the mind of the World. It wasn't sufficient to
be infected with the parasite for the transformation
to happen. That could make a human being sick,

nothing more. It was only when the polarity in the blood of the victim reached a certain level that the "phase transition" to magnetism occurred. Then the hunter and the hunted became one. Of course, once a human was fully transformed, he could change others simply with his blood. He would change them *rapidly*—more rapidly than the water could. He could take over a whole planet with his blood.

But these men would not give the World a chance to send its cells into their bodies to start the process. High up in the sky they sent forth a burst of light that exploded as it touched the World, rending the ground, carving out a crater where not a single one of the World's cells survived. Only then did the space ships slowly descend into the safe haven of the exploded crater. It was there that they began to erect their machine.

The World watched at first. It could do little more until the ones it had converted arrived on the scene. The men worked quickly. The thing they built began to take shape in less than a day. Yet it was not done at the end of the day, and the World waited until the sun had vanished to send forth its hungry legions. They came by the thousands. For eons the World had stored them up in the bowels of its caves, not just people from the third world, but visitors from faraway stars as well, changed beings who lived only to eat and serve the will of the World.

Once more the third world men had been warned. They never slept and were able to activate powerful red and green energy beams at the first sign of attack. These rays cut down the World's legions of walking and flying dead. In a short time there was nothing but millions of twitching limbs surrounding the crater the men had carved for themselves. Many of the limbs, driven by the will of the World, rose on their fingers and toes and wings to try to reach the enemy. But these, too, the men fired upon, and soon there was only smoking ash in place of what had once been the World's great defense.

But in the midst of this conflict one of the men grew careless and stepped beyond the confines of the crater. The World was on him in a moment, pushing its seed into his bloodstream. The man screamed as he was attacked, and the other men were warned. They didn't run to his aid; instead they fired their energy beams upon him without mercy. They'd had experience, the World thought. Before the men destroyed their partner, the World got a glimpse of the man's mind and understood that the machine the men were erecting was meant to rupture the crust of the World. It was a gigantic bomb. The men had come to kill the World. They wished to kill it because the transformed beings the World had sent back to the third planet had all but destroyed the human race. These men, the World saw, and a handful of others on the third planet were all that was left of a vast civilization, a culture that would now in all probability become extinct.

The World didn't know what to do. It could do nothing; the men were determined. The World watched as the men finished their machine the next day and then retreated into space. The World knew that the machine continued to tick; it could hear the sound of the machine's internal parts moving. It knew the countdown was on.

Then the mighty bomb exploded, and a deep pain shot through the mind of the World. A mushroom of fire appeared, and the World felt its insides scream. The men had accomplished their goal; the crust was ruptured. The spin of the World did the rest. Huge chunks of its body flew off into space. Then the incredible pressures at the center of the World were released, and the World exploded in a horrendous burst of energy, and the agony was beyond relief.

Until it stopped. The pain suddenly stopped.

The World was gone. It was dead. Lifeless rocks tumbled through the void where once the World had lived and eaten supreme.

Yet a few small pieces of the World survived, in a confused state. Those chunks of the world's crust held the cells of the World. They floated for eons with consciousness but no comprehension. They knew only their hunger, which they could no longer satisfy, and their hatred of the men who had destroyed their home. Above all else, they vowed that if there was ever a chance, they would take vengeance upon the people of the third planet.

In time it looked as if a few of the pieces were to be given that chance. Because as they tumbled through space, some pieces passed close to the third planet. Around and around the sun they went, until a few actually hit the planet. Of those, most landed in the vast oceans and were lost. But two hit the land, and once more there was great fire and pain for the feeble remnants of the World's once-vast mind. Almost all of the cells were destroyed in the heat of the landing, but a few lived in the rock that was eventually softened by the mighty glaciers. The glaciers left many lakes behind—the waters in which the cells eventually found release. There, in two small bodies of fresh water on the third planet, the cells multiplied and waited for the day they could once more cause the blood to flow in those who had destroyed their home. The sweet red blood, the only thing that truly satisfied the hunger.

"Angie," Kevin said.

Angela opened her eyes. She saw the ceiling of the basement, the exposed boards of the floor above, a single bulb burning bright. She smelled blood, the sour taste of copper in the air, and beneath that, the faint aroma of sweet iron. She moved her jaw and heard it crack. Her face was covered with gook; she could feel its dried stickiness stretch as her skin flexed. Blood, she thought. An angry heart pounded inside her skull. Every beat brought greater and greater pressure, demanding relief. She tried to sit up, and the pain went off the scale.

"Ouch," she moaned, squeezing her eyes shut and doubling up. Kevin held her a moment, trying to help her.

"Don't get up," he said. "Just sit. We don't have anywhere to go at the moment anyway."

She reopened her eyes to see she was sitting in a puddle of blood. It was caked over her face. Her fingers flew up to her head. She had a cut, a bad bruise at the back of her skull, but she couldn't have lost all the blood she was sitting in. She glanced at Kevin. He didn't look that much worse off for Jim's blow, although the left side of his face was puffy. He wasn't soaked in the stuff. What had they done to her? Poured a gallon of blood down her throat while she lay unconscious on her back? She had a horrible taste in her mouth. But it didn't rival the pounding inside her head. Nothing could touch that. She was going to have to eat something soon, or she was going to have to saw the top of her head open.

"How long have you been awake?" Angela asked, pulling the front of her shirt out of her pants and rubbing her face.

"Just a couple of minutes," Kevin said. His eyes strayed to the ceiling. "We're locked down here. They're still up there."

She listened. The boards creaked overhead. "I'm not surprised."

Kevin rubbed his head. "What the hell's going on? Do they blame us for the deaths of Todd and Kathy?"

"I doubt they're worried about that at the moment."

"Then why did they clobber the two of us? What

are they all doing here? Jim told me you were having a party."

"This is not a party," Angela said.

"I can see that. Tell me what's going on. Please?"

"We are being held captive by thirty vampires from outer space."

"Angie?"

"That's all I know." Her nightmare came back to her right then. The ruin of the ancient human civilization. The men's bomb. The death of the evil World. The asteroids' long tumble through time and space and the rebirth of the parasitic cells in the water of the two lakes. She added, "Don't ask me any more."

Kevin was impatient. "That's not good enough, Angie."

She winced in pain. "I'm sorry."

He was instantly regretful and reached out to touch her head. "We have to get you to a doctor," he said.

She was very aware of his hand on her skin. It was almost as if each one of the cells in the region where he was making contact had its own unique radar to detect different characteristics of his flesh. She was especially sensitive to the blood in his fingers, flowing beneath the surface of his skin. Such a frail sheet of skin—that simple layer of humanity that took only moments to peel away. . . .

The pounding in her head reached a feverish pitch.

She pushed his hand away.

"I'm all right," she said, getting up without his help. A wave of dizziness passed through her, but soon she was steady on her feet. The basement had no windows, of course; she knew that without checking. There was only one way out—the door up to the first floor of the house. She strode over to the corner where she had hidden her bottles of gasoline under a big blue plastic tarp. She pulled away the covering. The bottles were still there.

But the fuse was gone.

She searched in her pockets. They had taken her lighters.

"What's in those bottles?" Kevin asked. He was not stupid. The way they were roped together said she was not storing up fresh drinking water.

"Gasoline," she said.

His eyes widened. "Are they going to blow us up?"

"No," she said. "I was going to blow them up."

"Why, for godsakes?"

"For the sake of God," she told him. She understood right then that there was no getting away. The best she could hope for was to stop them. It was going to mean that both she and Kevin would die, and that made her sadder than she could bear. But it was the way it had to be. He was watching her with fear in his eyes.

"Have you lost your mind?" he asked.

"Kevin," she said sadly, "those people up there are evil. Mary was right—they kill others. There's no way to convince the authorities of what they're really like because for a long time they look like you and me. But they're not like us. They've got something growing in them that they've got to feed, that pushes them to take revenge against all of humanity. There's no way to stop them but to kill them."

"You sound as bad as Mary."

"Mary's dead," she cried.

He was shocked. "What happened?"

"They killed her."

He tried to hug her. "Angie?"

"Stay away," she said, pushing him aside a bit too hard. He almost fell down. She reminded herself how strong she had become. She seemed a lot stronger than she had been when Jim had arrived with Kevin tonight. Had they really poured blood down her throat? Whose blood had it been? Kevin was totally confused.

"What's wrong with you?" he pleaded.

"Right now I have many personal problems, but I can't go into all of them." She scanned the basement. There were the concrete walls and one wood-paneled—her grandfather never finished paneling the room. "Do you have any matches?" she asked quietly.

"No."

"Do you have a lighter?"

"I don't smoke, Angie. You're not going to try to light those bottles off."

She stared him straight in the eye. Once more, as in Mary's cabin, she felt a magnetic current flow up her spine, into her head, and out her eyes. The invisible mind-twister—she hoped it was working well this time.

"But I am, Kevin," she said softly. "That's exactly what I'm going to do. Now I want you to stand there and do nothing. I don't want you to interfere."

Suddenly he was breathing hard—sweating profusely. "You can't," he whispered.

"I can. I will. Don't interfere." She tore at a corner piece of the wood paneling. Tightening her fingers on the wood, she heard it crunch beneath the pressure of her grip. Her tendons felt like steel cords. She had broken off a three-foot section of splintered wood, which she snapped in two across her knee. One end looked like a jagged spear. She returned to her bottles in the corner and stabbed the nearest one. Gasoline gurgled onto the floor.

"Angie," Kevin croaked at her back, frozen in place.

"Shut up. Be still."

"You must stop."

"I'll stop when they're stopped," she said. She knelt and stood the jagged piece up in the middle of the growing puddle of gasoline. She gripped the top of it tightly with her left hand. In her right hand she held the second piece of wood. The monsters upstairs obviously had never been Boy Scouts or Girl Scouts, and didn't know all the games she knew. They had taken away her lighters—big deal. She needed just one good spark. She struck the piece of wood hard along the length of the other piece. She was strong—it would take only a few tries. She closed her eyes. It would be over soon.

But she weakened. She had driven herself within an inch of death, and perhaps the alien organism that flowed in her veins had even helped her so far. But the human part of her couldn't bear it. She was only eighteen. She didn't want to die. Certainly, she didn't want to die by her own hand. Tears burst out of her eyes, and the pieces of wood in her hands shook and fell into the gasoline. Blood and tears and gasoline; she tasted all three of them at once—a potion of despair.

"I can't," she moaned.

The next thing she knew, Kevin's arms were around her, comforting her. His gentle words in her ear told her everything was going to be all right. But his touch brought her no relief. It only hammered on the already unbearable pounding in her skull. He turned her toward him, and she smelled him a million times more intensely than the way she used to smell the meat on the barbecue when she was starving and it was almost, but not quite, ready to eat.

I am so ready, God.

"We'll get out of here," Kevin promised her.

She studied him—such a beautiful boy, so handsome. He had never really turned her on before, and now she couldn't imagine why not. She stroked his hair. She felt the bump where he had hit the wall. He had broken skin there. Taking a deep breath, she caressed the spot. It seemed to bring him pleasure, just her touching his head. He closed his eyes briefly. She withdrew the finger and licked it quickly with her tongue. A drop of blood, a pinch of pleasure. She touched his small wound again. She dug into it deeper this time, using her nails.

"Ouch," he said, drawing back slightly. His eyes popped open.

"I'm sorry," she said quickly. She had more blood on her hands now. But she couldn't lick it with him watching her—he wouldn't approve.

He stared at her. "You look different."

"You look good."

"Really?"

"Yeah," she croaked. His eyes were sort of bloodshot. She could count the veins around his irises. She could almost count the veins inside his pupils, the openings into his brain. She felt as if she could just reach out and touch his brain, squeeze it a little, she could make him feel a little better and herself a whole lot better. It was the thought of these *little* things that seemed to ease the pounding in her head. She really had to stop it from pounding, or else she was going to go mad. "Kiss me," she said suddenly.

"What?"

"Kiss me."

He chuckled. "Angie, we have to get out of here."

"I know. Kiss me." She grabbed him and pulled him closer. "Now."

He kissed her. He was not as aggressive as good old Jimmy boy. But he was sweet nevertheless. He kissed with more style, in a way, more flavor. She nibbled on his lip a tiny bit. He tasted just fine in her book. He drew back. He had blood on his mouth. My, my, where had that come from? It didn't look bad on him. He didn't need to wipe it away, but he did anyhow.

"You bit me," he said, looking at the back of his hand.

"I'm sorry," she panted. "Did it hurt?"

"No. But—"

"Kiss me again."

"I can't do it right now."

"Yes." She grabbed his head and pulled his lips onto hers. She sucked on them hungrily, and when he tried to pull away she didn't let him. The pleasure was exquisite, but the more she had, the more she wanted. They were sitting in a puddle of gasoline, but they were fanning the wrong kind of flames, the easy ones that did not require the courage to look death in the face.

This she knew. This she remembered.

Deep inside a warning bell finally went off. It told her that she was doing exactly what she had sworn that she would never do. But the bell could hardly compete with the pounding in her cranium. The bell was a drugstore-size alarm; the pounding was being rung by the hammer of Thor himself. Her need to feed drowned out everything else. She began to cry again even as she held on to him. She had told him to stay away. She had told him she just wanted to be friends. It was all his fault!

"Angie," he cried as he burst from her grasp. He

was breathing hard again; his eyes blinked rapidly. Half his face was smeared with blood. "What's wrong with you?" he demanded.

She spoke with feeling. "I just want you so much."

He forced a smile. "I feel like you're trying to take advantage of me."

She tried to smile. "I want to. I'm sorry."

"You don't have to be sorry."

"No?"

"No." He brushed away a tear from her cheek. "You're scared, but everything's going to be all right. I'm going to take care of you."

"Really?"

He grinned. "Really, A and W. There are no monsters."

"Thank God." She took his hands in hers and kissed them. Then she slipped her hands around the back of his neck, massaging him lightly at the base of the skull with her fingertips, relaxing him. Once more he closed his eyes. She didn't want him to open them again. She leaned forward and opened her mouth and kissed him once more, deeper than ever, so deep she felt she was inside him, a part of him, and that he was a part of her. Their two hearts beat inside each other in ecstasy. She wanted them to be that close. It was more than a physical craving; it was spiritual as well. It was meant to be; she could see that now. But she wasn't like the others, because she didn't want him to suffer. Not her dear Kevin. She just wanted to love him—to make him hers.

She tightened her grip on the back of his head.

"I love you, Kevin," she whispered.

I will always love you. Forever and ever.

She snapped his head around as hard as she could.

She heard the bones in his neck crack.

Not like at a chiropractic office, though.

Oh, no. Much louder cracks.

Kevin slumped in her arms.

He was no longer breathing hard. Not at all, really.

He was just asleep, she thought.

She brushed his hair from his face.

He could sleep as long as he liked.

She kissed his cheek. "Love you," she said.

She opened her mouth and closed her eyes.

She started. Her mind left her.

It was a good thing.

CHAPTER XIV ──

LIEUTENANT NGUYEN DROVE AIMLESSLY AROUND
Balton. He knew what he had to do. He had to go to
Angela's house and talk to her about Mary's story.
Nguyen had a feeling Angela believed Mary's story
now, and he also believed she had good reason to.
He was almost ready to believe it himself. But
Angela had told him to stay away from her. She had
ordered him somehow, deep inside his brain. He
felt compelled to speak with her, but he felt he'd be
committing the worst mistake of his life if he got
within ten miles of her.

He finally ended up stopping at Rest Lawn
Cemetery, where Todd Green and Kathy Baker had
been buried. It was close to eleven-thirty, and
naturally the place was locked up. But he kept a
lock-pick kit in his car and could spring any
common lock. Besides, if cops came by, he could
just flash his badge and tell them he was on police
business.

*I'm interrogating the murder victims. They might
have something to tell me, after all.*

Actually, he had no idea why he was at the

cemetery. But when the lock clicked open in his hands and the metal gate creaked as it swung clear of the entrance road, he felt a cold hand touch the base of his spine. He didn't want to be there any more than he wanted to be in the company of Angela Warner. He had seen many people die in his life—hundreds. He had walked by the torn corpses of recent comrades after a VC rocket strike and not felt as nervous as he did right then. He stepped inside the cemetery, and the cold slowly traveled up his spine to the region of his heart. He couldn't be free of the memory of the green stuff that had grown out of the blood of those two teenagers. When he had first entered Jim Kline's house after the shootings last week he had been overwhelmed with sorrow. Now he wondered if he shouldn't have felt relief that those two were dead.

The grave sites of Todd and Kathy weren't hard to find. It was a small cemetery, and the flowers from the funerals were still heaped up on the uneven dirt rectangles. The two had been buried next to each other. Nguyen sighed and sat down between them, where the grass still grew green. He asked himself once more why he was there.

He felt, in his indecision, that he was missing an important event.

He couldn't get Angela's words out of his mind: *"Quit following me. Let me do what I have to do. By the time you know enough to believe what is happening, you'll already be dead."*

What was Angela going to do? Take up where Mary had left off? Kill more of them? The monsters

209

with the green demons in their veins and the red blood in their mouths? The last time he had seen Angela she had been wiping away the blood that had spilled from her mouth. Whose side was she on?

A breeze came up, moaning as it passed through the branches of nearby trees. Yet the moan did not stop when the wind ceased. The sound seemed to carry across the cemetery, to come in waves, like the moan that would come from a living human being if he or she were in pain. Sitting where he was, Nguyen's heart began to pound silently.

The moaning was not coming from the wind.

It was coming from beside him.

Below him.

"Save us, Lord Buddha," he whispered.

Nguyen leaned over and cocked his head above the grave of Todd Green. He didn't actually put his ear to the soil, which would have been the best procedure to follow if the moan were truly coming from under the ground and he wanted to verify that fact. He had a fear—it was ridiculous, but then again, so was what he was hearing—that a hand might reach up out of the soil and grab him and pull him under. Or at least pull off his ear. Tran Quan, that tyrant in his company in Nam, collected the ears of the VC he had killed. Once Nguyen had seen him cut off the ears of one of their own dead soldiers. Nguyen had always had a thing about losing his own ears.

The moaning came again.

"Jesus," Nguyen whispered. He always called

upon both Buddha and Jesus when things got really bad.

The groan was coming from *far* under the ground —like six feet under. Nguyen told himself that the only thing down there was a box with Todd Green's corpse in it, and that this was not possible. The groan did not sound fully human, though that did nothing to comfort him. Rather, it sounded more like some kind of huge, hungry animal.

Nguyen leapt to his feet and took twenty quick steps away from the grave site. There he could no longer hear the sound. That was good. It had never been there to begin with, he thought. He had imagined it.

But then Nguyen made himself take the twenty steps back to Todd's grave, and he heard the moan again. "Stop," he screamed at the ground.

The moan stopped.

Todd's corpse had heard and understood him.

Nguyen turned and ran to his car. He started the engine and pulled away from the cemetery at high speed. He had to see Angela Warner, human or not. He had to talk to her. He realized he might have to kill her.

If she could still be killed.

211

— CHAPTER XV —

THEY OPENED THE DOOR TO THE BASEMENT NEAR THE time she finished feeding. For some reason the light in the basement had failed, and she had had to satisfy her hunger in darkness. The shaft of light from upstairs stung her eyes. They were up there— she could see them staring down at her. Somebody named Jim was at the front of the pack.

"We are going to have a meeting," the one called Jim said.

She stood and saw she was soaked in blood. It was everywhere around her, dripping off small chunks of torn flesh. She couldn't remember exactly where it had come from, but it had been good— the blood and the flesh. She could also remember the pounding in her head, but that had stopped, which was also good. The pounding had been painful. She walked to the steps.

"I will come to your meeting," she said.

"Clean up first," the one named Jim said.

"I will clean up first," she said.

She went up the stairs, and then up another flight to a room she recognized. It was called bedroom, and it belonged to a human called Angela Warner. She knew Angela—she was Angela. She was that body. It was the body and the clothes on the body that had to be cleaned up. She was alone in the room but knew what to do. It was called shower, which she could do in the place called shower. That was in the bathroom, which was over there. She understood these things—sort of. First the blood had to come off.

The water came out warm, and it reminded her of the blood. She did not need any blood right now but knew she'd need some later. The need would always be there, but as long as there was blood, the painful pounding would stay away. The meeting could be about finding more blood. When she was clean she'd go to the meeting.

The water washed away the blood. When she stepped out of the shower she saw a thing called robe. Angela Warner would put on the robe after shower, so she put on the robe. It was yellow, and her hair was wet as she looked in the mirror. There was no blood. Angela Warner would smile when she looked in the mirror, so she smiled. The smile showed her teeth, which she'd use the next time she needed blood.

There was something sitting on the counter of the bathroom in front of the mirror. It was called picture. She picked it up; a picture of people. She recognized the bodies: Angela Warner, Mary Blanc, Kevin Jacobs. They were holding one another and smiling. They were—she had trouble with the word, but it came at last—happy. Happy bodies.

She knew the word, but not the meaning. But she believed happy meant the pounding had stopped and that there was blood. She decided she was happy. Happy and clean.

There was something else on the countertop. It was the color gold and shaped like a KAtuu minus its head. She knew what a KAtuu was. She was KAtuu. She was part of the World. Angela Warner's body would change into this shape KAtuu as time passed. If there was enough blood. It took a lot of blood, many killings, to become a full KAtuu. She knew that. It was her destiny.

But she didn't know why she suddenly put the amulet over her head.

It may have been she had another destiny.

Even now—so late.

A powerful tremor passed through her body. Her mind, her connection to the World and all the KAtuu that were and had ever been, was suddenly made visible in her being. A ghostly red ribbon circled the house and all the KAtuu that were gathered there; it streamed off into the sky and then deep into space, out to where the surviving cells of the World tumbled forever on the surface of misshapen asteroids in the endless black of the abyss. They called to her, and she called to them. They desperately wanted her to stay a part of them and bring the flow of blood among the enemy that had destroyed the World.

But something else also called, in a voice that belonged to the body alone. It was the voice of Angela Warner's thoughts. It was the sound of

Angela's heart, beating deep inside the body; pounding, not like the pain in the head when the blood was not available, but throbbing with the feelings of the enemy.

But who was the enemy?

Who had invaded whom?

They invaded us.

Us. Humans.

The red ribbon turned a ghastly purple and began to dissolve along the endless road back to Earth. Then it suddenly snapped, and Angela drew in a sharp breath.

Yes, Angela Warner. She remembered who she was, *what* she was. Not KAtuu, not even with the horrors she had committed. She was human. She was not the enemy. They were. They were evil.

"Kevin," she whispered. Tears formed in her eyes; she saw them in the mirror. But she didn't allow them to flow onto her cheeks. Kevin was dead—she couldn't worry about him now. She couldn't think about what she had done to him, or she'd go insane before she could finish her job.

But that was easier to say than do. Nausea swept over her, and she turned to the toilet and vomited red junk that made her keep vomiting until there was nothing left in her guts. She hoped to God there was nothing left.

"Kevin," she cried softly.

The pounding began to throb inside her brain.

This time she welcomed it.

Angela whirled and ran to her bedroom closet. Earlier she'd had trouble tying the smaller bottles of gasoline in a circle with the other five-gallon bottles. She had finally decided not to put all her eggs in one basket. She had stacked her eight two-and-a-half-gallon bottles behind the clothes in her closet. Because she had gone and buried her grandfather's remains after all, she had not had time to make herself a second fuse. Her second basket was a last-resort bomb. She had figured if she had to light it, she would probably be going up with it.

The bottles of gasoline were where she had left them.

It was past the time for last resorts, she decided.

Angela closed the closet door and began to rifle through her desk for a lighter. Luck was with her. She found a bag holding three new ones: red, white, and blue. A choice of colors. Ripping open the plastic, she grabbed the red one.

The plastic.

The dog was standing on the balcony, peering in through the screen door with fear in her eyes. If she blew up the house, Angela thought, she would kill Plastic. A small price to pay for the safety of the human race, to be sure, but she already felt bad for what she had earlier done to the dog. She hurried to the screen door and quietly opened it. Plastic was forgiving. The dog immediately began to lick Angela's hands and whimper as Angela knelt beside her.

"Shh," Angela said softly. "You can't stay here. You have to go swim." She pointed. "Jump in the water. Go swim, that a girl. Go Plastic. Get the hell out of here."

Of course, Plastic didn't jump in the lake. The dog had never liked the water and wasn't about to start liking it. Angela was debating what to do next when she saw Jim come through her bedroom door. He was alone. She glanced at the closet. She had closed the door but had not shut it.

"We are going to start the meeting," Jim said tonelessly.

Angela let go of the dog and stood. She tried to keep her voice and face expressionless. "I am coming," she said.

"Come now."

She stepped into the bedroom. Plastic remained on the balcony. "I need to dress more," she said.

"It does not matter," Jim said, watching her. "The meeting will start now."

"I will be down in a minute," she said, wondering if the KAtuu ever argued among themselves. Her eyes darted to the open drawer of her desk, then back to Jim. She had left the torn packet of lighters sitting on top of a box of unsharpened pencils. The red lighter, of course, she had hidden in the fingers of her left hand. She was in a quandary; she didn't want to move in the direction of the desk and draw Jim's attention to it, but she remembered she had left her hunting knife in the top drawer on the right. The way Jim was staring at her, she might need that knife very soon.

"What is that you're wearing?" he asked.

Damn! The amulet.

"What?" she asked. She could feel the gold chain around her neck and didn't have to lower her eyes to look at the amulet. She began to edge toward the desk.

"What is that you're wearing around your neck?" he repeated.

"It is decoration," she said. Another step toward the desk. Jim turned his whole body to follow her. He took a step closer.

"It looks like K.Atuu," he said.

"Yes."

"Where did you get it?" he asked.

"What?"

"Who gave you that amulet?" he asked.

She finally looked at it; she touched its gold surface and said a silent prayer of thanks to Shining Feather. If she was going to die, at least she was going to die human.

"An Indian," she said.

"When?" He was close now, maybe two steps away.

"Just now," she said.

"I do not understand," Jim said. "Where is this Indian?"

"I will show you." She strode toward the closet, passing within inches of the desk. But she didn't reach for the knife—not yet. One hand on the door of the closet, she said, "He is hiding in here."

Jim quickly stepped by her and threw open the door of the closet. In that same moment Angela took a step back, pulled open the desk drawer, and grabbed the knife with her right hand. The stacked bottles of gasoline had distracted Jim just enough for her to accomplish that small maneuver. But Jim had ears, he had reflexes. He was whirling to confront her when she snapped back the knife and stabbed the razor-sharp blade into the side of his neck.

"Help!" he shouted as a fountain of blood erupted over his shoulder. The blood was darker than it should have been; it had a distinct green tinge to it. She had lost the knife in her attack. He reached up with both hands to pull it free as he staggered back a step. She lashed out with her foot, with every bit of her newfound strength, and caught him directly in the balls. He grunted and bent over, and the blood from his neck dripped onto the floor.

"Bastard!" she swore.

She ran to the bedroom door and slammed it shut. They were already coming up the stairs. She twisted the lock into place. She did not think that it would hold them long, and she was right. Their first blow on the door brought the sound of splintering wood.

Angela hurried back to the closet. She had to jump over Jim in the process. He had fallen to the floor. He feebly reached up to grab her leg but failed. He was swiftly losing strength. His blood formed a pool around him, and she briefly wondered how many poor souls' blood had gone into his veins to make that weird puddle.

"Help," he gasped.

The door shook again. They would be inside in seconds.

Angela opened the closet door and grabbed the top bottle of gasoline. She dropped it on the floor in front of her, jumped in the air, and landed on it with both feet. The plastic walls burst; the gasoline spilled over the floor of the bedroom and the closet, around the stack of plastic bottles. The fuel also splattered the hem of her robe. She whipped up her left hand and flipped her Bic. The orange flame glowed like a tiny sun in her eyes. She looked down at Jim. He was watching her.

"You waited a hundred thousand years for revenge," she said. "You wasted your time. You're goners. You're just a bunch of dead heads from a dead world." She paused and smiled wickedly. "I hope you feel pain when you die."

With that Angela leaned over and lit the edge of the puddle of gasoline. It caught immediately; the flames raced into the closet and engulfed her wardrobe and the bottles of gasoline. Her robe had also caught fire, but she didn't stop to try to put it out. Her bedroom door lurched; a huge chunk of wood came smashing in behind the power of an angry fist. Angela turned and ran toward the door to the balcony.

It was fortunate she had left the door open.

Angela had scarcely crossed the threshold to the outside when two things happened almost simultaneously. The bedroom door burst open, and the front ranks of the gang of vampires barged in. They had only a split second to survey their fallen leader and the fire in the closet before her alternative bomb exploded.

Angela experienced the shock wave as the slap of a giant's unforgiving hand, a slap that literally swept her off her feet and off the balcony. She was immediately blinded by the brilliant light. But this was a hand that could strike more than once. A second shock wave hit her as she hovered above the lake. At the back of her mind she registered the fact that the power of the explosion upstairs had been sufficient to burst through to the basement and ignite the larger bomb.

All sixty gallons had gone up. Whew.

Then a *third* shock wave hit her, and this one made the other two puny by comparison. She was in the sky, flying toward the moon—anywhere but toward the asteroid belt—and she still understood what had happened. The propane tank had blown. No one, she thought, *nothing* could have survived that. The fact reassured what was left of her mind and body as she reached the upward arc of her flight and began to fall, down into the cold black waters where it had all begun, and where it would now all end.

Lieutenant Nguyen was two hundred yards from Angela Warner's house when it exploded. First the top blew off, then a geyser erupted from deep inside, and finally the white tank beside the house went up like a miniature atomic bomb. A mushroom cloud of fire reached for the stars. Nguyen immediately pulled over to the side of the road. He thought he glimpsed a figure on fire kicking and yelling as it flew out over the lake. But then he blinked and the figure was gone, and he didn't hear a splash. Had he imagined it?

Nguyen got out of his car, stood in the suddenly hot night, and watched the house burn. He didn't use his radio to call for help. He imagined everyone in the town of Point had heard the explosion. Plus he wanted the place to burn as long as possible. The people who were inside—he wanted them turned to ash, because that's what Angela must have wanted. He knew it was she who had stopped them, and even though he didn't fully understand what they were, he knew they had been horrible enough.

In the orange light of the fire Nguyen lowered his head and silently saluted Mary Blanc and Angela Warner.

EPILOGUE

Three Months Later

LIEUTENANT NGUYEN WALKED THE SHORE OF POINT
Lake not far from where Angela Warner's house
had stood. Although the fire had been before the
winter had come and the snow had fallen, there
were still signs of that horrible night to be found.
The snow had covered most of what remained of
the charred wood, but the black skeleton of a
support beam still stuck up through the white
blanket, and a few boards from the balcony bal-
anced precariously on the stilts of scarred wood
that wouldn't stand the next strong windstorm.

Nguyen made no effort to get too close to the
house, however. It might have been a place of
triumph—he still believed that—but it held un-
pleasant memories for him. He had been present
when the bodies of the thirty-two Point High
students had been removed from the wreckage. Of
course, they had not known then that there had
been thirty-two people at Angela's house when it
blew. There had not been a single intact corpse.

But there were experts for every task in the
world, even the gruesome ones, and maybe morti-

cian Kane had come to lend a hand. In any case, the burnt remains had been gathered, and the teenagers had been numbered and identified, mostly using dental records. Jim Kline, Larry Zurer, Carol McFarland—the list went on and on. Nguyen had been surprised and saddened to discover Kevin Jacobs had also been killed. According to the experts, he had been the only one in the basement when the explosion occurred. There had not been enough of him left to bury.

No remains had been found of Angela Warner though.

Not even in the water. Nguyen had made them search there.

"Don't, girl," Nguyen called to his dog. She had belonged to Angela and her grandfather; Nguyen had found her wandering around the night of the blowup, soaking wet and deaf. The dog had yet to regain all its hearing. Kids at the school, classmates of Angela's, had told her the dog's name was Plastic. Nguyen called her that sometimes. "Don't get oil on your paws," he said. "Stay away from the water."

Nguyen had come to say goodbye to the area. He was moving to California. Many people were leaving; Point was quickly becoming a ghost town. The trauma from the deaths of so many kids had shattered families beyond repair. They couldn't bear to live and breathe in the same place that had brought them so much grief.

Then there was the strange story of the oil spill.

Approximately six weeks after the explosion a gentleman by the name of Phillip Frazier was attacked while driving his company truck——a full-size propane tanker that was in the area refueling tanks for the approaching winter. Mr. Frazier was unable to explain afterward what had attacked him, except to say that it had come at him from the *roof* of the cab and that it was stronger and faster than anything he had ever seen. In fact, he said it was so fast he didn't even see it. The police thought that unlikely, but he stuck to his story.

Mr. Frazier had been knocked unconscious in the attack, and his truck had been stolen. It didn't take long for the truck to be relocated, however. That evening, just after sunset, the wells that pumped on the hills overlooking Point Lake exploded. It seemed the thief had driven the truck up to the wells, probably coming at them from behind, and had detonated the propane tank in the midst of the small oil field. Two of the wells had immediately caught fire, and before help could arrive all six were burning out of control. It was like the Kuwait oil fields after the Gulf War all over again. Experts had to be brought in from the Middle East to extinguish the wells, and that took several days. Even more unfortunate, the burning wells served as cover for a much greater catastrophe.

There were six pumping wells on the hill. In addition, there were another six wells that pro-duced a tremendous amount of oil without being pumped; the natural gas pressure underground was enough to drive the oil to the surface. These six wells, and the holding tanks that stored their oil, were also ruptured by the explosion of the propane truck. But they didn't catch fire. Their tank lines were broken, however, and the oil spilled ceaselessly into Point Lake for several days, a black river hidden by the flames of the other wells. Naturally, locals noticed the oil building up in the lake before the other wells were extinguished, but it wasn't possible to dam the flow properly until the flames had been put out. By then Point Lake had absorbed an oil spill that was irreparable. The cost to clean it up was put in the tens of millions by state experts, and it was decided the lake would be drained the coming spring. Drained and covered over; it wouldn't do to have such a huge tar pit lying exposed.

So Point was a dead town. Better to get out while the getting was good, people were saying. Nguyen agreed. He had other reasons as well.

He knew he was going to have to get rid of whatever was sleeping in Todd Green's grave before he left. It was a task he wasn't looking forward to.

"Come on, Plastic," he called as he stepped away from the oily shore and headed into the trees. The collie followed happily, wagging her tail. At first Plastic had clearly missed Angela and her grandfather, but dogs quickly forgot. They were lucky. "Let's go see if we can find any game."

The snow crunched under Nguyen's boots as

they hiked into the woods. The light was poor—it was close to sunset. He should have come earlier, he thought. The ground turned upward; he had to veer to the south to stay away from the place where the oil had burned and flowed. Climbing the hills was hard work in the soft snow. Nguyen found himself panting and had to take numerous breaks, even though he was in excellent shape. His constant searching also made him tire more quickly than normal. He had come to say good-bye to the area but also was looking for something he'd seen many times before—ever since the night the thirty-two kids had died in Angela Warner's house.

Nguyen was searching for the remains of a dead animal.

He found one a few minutes later.

They weren't that hard to find if you knew where to search.

The animal was a deer—a doe. There wasn't much of it left. It had been completely gutted by what appeared to be a combination of teeth and knives. Bright red blood soaked into the surrounding snow. The vacant eyes of the deer stared up at him. He doubted the animal had even gotten a glimpse of what had killed it.

Nguyen had believed Phillip Frazier's story.

"No, girl," Nguyen snapped as Plastic tried to lick the blood. "That's bad stuff. Stay away from it. Make you very sick."

The dog peered up at him quizzically for a

moment, then appeared to understand. She turned to chase after something else.

Suddenly the collie froze, its tail going straight up. But the dog did not raise it as a prelude to attack. Plastic whimpered softly. She was terrified.

"What is it, girl?" Nguyen whispered. He searched the woods but saw nothing. Nevertheless, a film of sweat began to gather on his skin beneath his woolen shirt. He remembered the coldness in Jim Kline's eyes; Angela licking Mary's blood; the stink of the green fungus in Kane's laboratory; the groan under the ground in Rest Lawn Cemetery. A collage of the unexplainable floated on the still air, mixed with the smell of evil. He remembered his glimpse of the burning figure being blasted out over the cold water when the house had exploded. No remains of Angela Warner—no one seemed to know where she had gone.

Nguyen glanced down at the empty eye of the doe. This was the tenth animal he had discovered eviscerated in these woods in the last six weeks.

All these memories. They made him ask himself questions.

What was out there? What was watching him?

Something.

Then, an even more important question.

Why had he come to these woods so close to dark?

Foolish.

Nguyen turned back to the lake, back the way he had come. He put a hand on the gun under his coat. It was a futile gesture. He knew he wouldn't have time to use it if he needed to. He called to Angela's dog.

"Let's get out of here, girl," he said.

High in a nearby tree red eyes watched the man and the animal depart. The mind behind the eyes was tempted. For a moment it considered attacking, swooping down from its branch and taking what it wished. But it hesitated. It had just eaten; it was not overly hungry. And there was something about the man, about people in general. The creature didn't know if it wanted to feed in that way.

The creature raised a purple talon to touch the figure at the end of the gold chain that hung around its wrinkled neck, then resettled its leathery wings on the thick branch where it sat. It did not understand why it always did this when it spotted human beings. It had no memory of where the amulet had come from. It had no memory at all, not even of the fifth planet from the sun that had supposedly given birth to it. It had broken the link to that place at the beginning. The creature simply existed and fed while time passed.

But as it touched the amulet with its sharp claws it came to a clear decision not to attack the man. There was something wrong about killing humans. The creature jingled the amulet, and as it did a faint wave of sorrow touched its mind. It could remember that much. People were not for eating.

Look for Christopher Pike's

Road to Nowhere

Coming in March 1993

---

and

Look for Christopher Pike's

The Eternal Enemy

Coming in May 1993

About the Author

CHRISTOPHER PIKE was born in Brooklyn, New York, but grew up in Los Angeles, where he lives to this day. Prior to becoming a writer, he worked in a factory, painted houses, and programmed computers. His hobbies include astronomy, meditating, running, playing with his nieces and nephews, and making sure his books are prominently displayed in local bookstores. He is the author of *Last Act, Spellbound, Gimme a Kiss, Remember Me, Scavenger Hunt, Final Friends* 1, 2, and 3, *Fall into Darkness, See You Later, Witch, Die Softly, Bury Me Deep, Whisper of Death, Chain Letter 2: The Ancient Evil, Master of Murder,* and *Monster,* all available from Archway Paperbacks. *Slumber Party, Weekend, Chain Letter, The Tachyon Web,* and *Sati*—an adult novel about a very unusual lady—are also by Mr. Pike.